SKEPTIC IN A SKIRT

LOVE EVER AFTER, BOOK 2

CATE LAWLEY

Copyright © 2019 Catherine G. Cobb
All rights reserved.
Previously published as *Timely Love* Copyright © 2016.

ABOUT SKEPTIC IN A SKIRT

Magic nevermore

Beth hasn't believed in magic since she was a small child. Meeting her very own wand-wielding fairy godmother doesn't change her mind. While she's always hoped for a special someone, she's pretty darn sure he won't be delivered by a delusional woman waving a wand.

Enter Edward, the man who lives in Beth's dreams. The *ideal* man. Perfectly handsome, perfectly kind, perfectly yummy smelling—perfectly not from this century.

Edward wants to believe in the helping hand of a

magical fairy. He certainly believes Beth is his One True Love.

Previously published in 2016, Skeptic in a Skirt *(formerly* Timely Love) *features almost entirely new content.*

1

BETH

Best. Dream. Ever.

I was dressed in a gorgeous gown. And by gown, truly a *gown*. Never in my life had I worn a floor-length dress, let alone one made of a champagne-colored fabric so fine that the material alone probably cost more than my used Corolla, and that didn't even take into account the embroidered and beaded detail that was clearly hand-stitched.

And I would know—about the cost, the hand stitching, the fabric, everything—because my BFF Hillary was a professional shopper with excellent taste and a need to share all things fashion with her bestie.

What gown was complete without accessories? Or so the dream version of myself had decided, because I was decked out.

Gloves covered my forearms, past my elbow to the middle of my almost nonexistent bicep. (Someone needed to get to the gym more often.) The cool weight of a necklace rested against my neck. A flash of brilliance at my wrist had me wondering if I was sporting a matched set, and if I was—wow. If I wasn't dreaming, I'd be worried about getting mugged, even standing in a rose-scented garden with the gentle murmur of polite conversation and classical music trickling in from the distance.

Paranoid much? Nope. The stones on my wrist looked expensive. As in house-down-payment pricey. Big sapphires surrounded by diamonds, and there they were, hanging out on my wrist, looking fabulous.

I knew my jewelry, and this bracelet was gorgeous, vintage, and not crystal. I even had a rough estimate of its worth in my head. Like I said, house-down-payment-level wow, and that was just the bracelet.

My deep and abiding love of jewelry was a dark secret I kept squirreled away from Hillary. She'd have me "investing" in period pieces in two seconds flat. I was practical; she wasn't. I was a planner; she wasn't. I loved rice cakes; she loved Funyuns. I had a retirement account; she had four struggling businesses.

We were opposites, not in the ways that really

mattered when it came to being friends, but certainly when it came to men, money, and work.

But if Hills ever discovered my love of jewelry... I shuddered. She'd have my fiscally cautious side in detention, and I'd buy *all* the sparkly things. I wasn't usually susceptible to her spontaneous, Funyuns-eating influence, but throw a little bling in front of me and the combination of my bestie and my biggest weakness would be too much.

Speaking of sparklies, the piece of jewelry encircling my wrist begged for further inspection, admiration, and maybe a little stroking and petting.

I blamed my love of sparkly things and the exquisite beauty of the particular piece I was examining for my inattentiveness. Also, hello? Dream. Who paid attention in dreams?

That was why the voice caught me so off guard.

Two simple words: "Pardon me."

I turned. All right, I tried to turn, but floor-length gowns and I have never been on a first-name basis, and it didn't go well.

Strong arms and a spicy, woodsy scent enveloped me.

Did dreams smell good?

Whatever. I was dreaming, and my dream smelled amazing.

He smelled amazing.

"Excuse me."

That voice. My insides might have melted.

"Are you unwell?" the man attached to the very nice arms asked. *He* probably made it to the gym five days a week.

Wait...

Dreams didn't have lovely smells, nice arms, or British accents.

2

EDWARD

She was a vision.

A clumsy vision, but beautiful. And I could hardly take exception to her lack of grace, since it was that very quality that had landed her within my embrace.

The lovely stranger was tall, perhaps five inches shorter than me when she'd been standing. Her height was appealing, as I towered over most women.

She smelled of exotic spices. Good enough to eat, certainly to nibble. Perhaps just there, below the curve of her jaw. Better yet, her lips, which parted with a breathy exhalation.

I cleared my throat. "Are you unwell?"

Since she had yet to untangle herself from her

own skirts, perhaps the lovely lady in my arms had no lack of grace, but rather had taken ill.

She blinked, drawing attention to her eyes. Blue. Not startlingly or brilliantly so. Perhaps even a little grayish, but they were fringed with surprisingly dark lashes, given her fair complexion.

She inhaled, and the grasp of her fingers on my upper arms tightened. "I need to get to the gym more often."

Her words made no sense, which supported my belief that she was unwell.

I scanned the area for a bench, discovered one ten feet away, then picked her up and gathered her close to my chest. For all her height, she didn't weigh much at all.

A disturbing thought intruded. This woman whose name I didn't know, who had uttered only a few words—none of which made sense—felt as if she belonged exactly where she was: in my arms.

3

BETH

I woke up and went to work.

Realistic or not, a dream was a dream was a dream, and this lady had bills to pay. Actually, my bills were under control, but I was working on a down payment for a house, and it was never too early to contribute to retirement savings.

I was a freelancer, and "going to work" involved me sitting down at my kitchen table, but the point was that I rolled out of bed and got right to it. I didn't think about that bizarrely realistic dream more than once or...

Who was I kidding?

That dream haunted me all day long.

My clients were important. They were the heart of my business. Making them happy by providing an exceptional work product was integral to The Plan.

Step one: find good clients.

Step two: make myself indispensable to my clients by rocking their world with my attention to detail, timeliness, and high-level problem-solving.

Step three: leverage the above to keep current clients and find new ones.

Nothing revolutionary, but The Plan was in motion, and it was working.

Small problem: I wasn't sticking to the master plan today. Doing exceptional work—any work—was a teensy bit difficult when I had a mystery man on the brain.

A mystery man who liked to dress in period clothing, worked out enough to have drool-worthy arms—I enjoyed squeezable biceps; it was a weakness—and didn't exist in reality.

What real man swept a woman off her feet, literally, these days?

Too bad I'd woken up before anything more exciting than being cuddled by a scrumptious, yummy-smelling hero could happen. It certainly hadn't qualified as a sex dream. We hadn't even kissed, sadly.

Maybe a flirtation dream?

But we'd barely spoken and certainly hadn't managed any flirtatious banter. Wasn't that what flirting was? Sexually charged banter between two mutually attracted individuals?

Or so I'd heard. If I'd ever flirted with a man, it had been by accident. Did I mention I'm very, very shy?

I cringed when I remembered the gist of the words I had managed to get out. Something about a need to get to the gym. I'd had two boyfriends, and I still considered both of them small miracles. Mostly because when confronted by scrumptious men, I did weird things. Blurting out a need to hit the gym didn't even make the top twenty list of weird things I'd done in front of hot guys.

Conclusion: my encounter with the mystery man had *not* been a flirtation dream.

Which left...the meet cute.

I'd had a G-rated, 1950s-style meet-cute dream.

Nifty. Leave it to me to have a non-sex sex dream.

I'd been watching too many old films. Maybe it was time to up the steam factor of my late-night movie-watching.

That was what Hillary would tell me.

I snorted.

As if I'd listen to Hillary's advice when it came to anything sex, man, or relationship related. I might be shy when it came to romance and men, but that girl had her own issues. She was a walking cliché. She was the female version of the mid-twenties man-child, flitting from relationship to relationship, unwilling to engage on any deep emotional level, and terrified of anything with a whiff of commitment attached.

No, late-night Cinemax wasn't in my future.

Besides, I never remembered my dreams. This one was an anomaly, so I probably wouldn't have another. There was no point in even considering future dreams with a specific, delicious man in period costume.

He really had filled out that suit nicely...

4

EDWARD

My mysterious beauty disappeared.

She was in my arms, clinging to me, her breath a whisper of warmth on my neck, then she was gone. Vanished, as if she'd never been.

Her existence, however, was a certainty. I had proof.

When I'd come upon her, she'd been examining her bracelet. The clasp must have been faulty, because when I picked her up, it fell from her wrist to the ground. The sapphire and diamond piece was striking, expensive, and *not* a figment of my imagination.

For two weeks, I increased my attendance at social functions. For two weeks, I searched for my mystery lady. She failed to appear at any event I attended, and the discreet inquiries I made regarding a certain beautiful, willowy blonde wearing a stunning sapphire necklace yielded no results.

It was as if she had never been.

But...I had the bracelet. That, and I carried the memory of her with me. Her spicy, exotic scent and the feel of her in my arms.

Since my sister's death a few years ago, I'd retreated from the social whirl. In the past, I'd attended various events to make her happy. But with Abigail gone, I had little reason to participate. I had only attended the event two weeks prior as a favor to an old friend of my sister's.

When Abigail fell ill, she'd expressed her concerns. She wished me to marry, but feared that without her influence I'd meet no one suitable. I preferred to wander the countryside and sketch, and she'd admonished me that I was unlikely to meet my match in such surroundings.

She'd been convinced there was a woman out in the world who was my match, but said I would only meet her if I ventured into society.

One woman, she'd teased, because I was a contrary, standoffish man who would need a very special woman indeed.

Would Abigail have thought me mad to search for a woman I'd met one time?

I thought not. She'd been a poet with a romantic soul.

Abigail would likely have encouraged me to search. To gamble my time and effort that perhaps this woman was the one, my match. To, at a minimum, investigate the possibility of a romantic connection.

And as I wearied of the social round, I told myself there was also the bracelet. It was a valuable item, and I felt obligated to perform due diligence in finding its owner.

But two weeks passed without even a hint of the mysterious blonde.

Hope was a fragile thing, and it lived for that two weeks but not longer.

That was when I returned to the regular rhythm of my life, a life devoid of parties, teas, and galas.

I no longer wandered the countryside, because I lived in town year-round now. Instead, I strolled through the parks until I found a suitable subject for my sketches. I'd discovered a fondness for wildflowers most recently.

Two weeks later, the sapphire bracelet was removed from my pocket and tucked away in my office, my hope for another meeting with my mystery lady nearly extinguished, and that was when I saw her.

Not at a dinner with tedious talk or a ball with matchmaking mamas.

I found her walking in one of my favorite parks.

Her walking costume was in no way inappropriate. Hair, hat, gloves, and parasol—all in perfect order. And yet there was an air of...otherness about her. Eyes wide, she cemented this impression when she twirled in a bewildered circle.

Our last encounter still fresh in my memory, I hurried to her side and arrived just in time to lend a steadying hand under her elbow.

"You!"

I hadn't expected thanks, but her accusatory tone was a surprise.

Once I was certain she was no longer in danger of falling, I stepped back and—reluctantly—removed my hand. "Pardon the impertinence. Edward Stanbury, at your service." I touched the brim of my hat.

"Edward." She tested my name as if it was foreign to her. And yet I knew she spoke English. An oddly inflected, curious sort of English.

I waited in hopes she'd share her own name, but she stood staring, her lips slightly parted and her eyebrows drawn together. My mystery lady appeared confused, startled, bothered—by me?

But then I remembered I held in my possession

an article of great value belonging to the lady. "I have your bracelet." For some unknown reason, I patted my coat pockets. I knew very well her jewels were locked in my office desk and not on my person. "Not with me, but secured, waiting to be returned to you."

She shook her head. "My bracelet?"

Clearly not the source of her consternation. "The sapphire and diamond bracelet you lost two weeks ago at the Smiths' gathering?"

"The Smiths?" She blinked several times, surveyed our surroundings—thankfully, only sparsely occupied at this time of day—and then examined her rust-colored walking dress.

Both seemed to cause her some distress.

"Where am I?" she asked in a hushed voice.

I responded with the name of the somewhat unfashionable park, and then I tucked her gloved hand under my arm and said, "Shall we walk?"

She nodded, and we walked together silently for several minutes.

A woman alone in a park without knowledge of how she came to be there was no stranger than her appearance in the Smiths' garden, where she appeared to have gone unnoticed by other attendees and simply vanished into thin air.

There was no reasonable explanation for her disappearance from the Smiths' garden. Everything else could be explained away with some creative thinking, but not that. And yet...

I knew she was real.

I knew she was a woman with whom I wished to better acquaint myself.

I knew I felt drawn to her in a way that was as yet unexplainable.

"What's the date?" Her fingers tightened on my arm. "Edward...what day is it?"

"Thursday." I considered her question and elaborated: "The eighteenth."

She frowned.

"May," I continued.

She took a deep breath. "And the year?"

The lovely blonde woman on my arm chewed on her lower lip in a very unladylike way.

"Eighteen ninety-nine."

"Right. Why not?" She stopped and turned to face me. Then she extended her hand. Once I accepted, she shook mine firmly and said, "I'm Beth Lind, and you're a dream."

I tucked her hand under my arm again. "Do I feel like a dream?"

She squeezed my forearm. "No." Then she added, much more softly, "And you don't smell like one, either."

It seemed ungentlemanly to call attention to the bold comment, so I turned the conversation to a topic I very much wished to pursue: Beth Lind. "Are you visiting the area?"

She considered the question and finally said, "Yes?"

"May I ask from where?"

"Austin, Texas. Um, the United States." After a brief hesitation, she asked, "Are you from...here?"

Texas—a reasonable explanation for her unusual accent. "My family is from the south of England, but I've lived in and around London since my parents passed away many years ago. My sister preferred town life."

"Oh, you have a sister. I always wanted one. I'm an only child." She tipped her head to the side. "I have a best friend who's almost like a sister, Hillary."

My sister had been my best friend, but her loss and my lack of close friends after her passing weren't topics upon which I wished to dwell. "My sister has also since passed."

"This place, these clothes—none of it's real. *You* can't be real. Except..." She stopped and closed her eyes. When she opened them again, they were overly bright. "I'm so sorry for your loss." She pulled her gaze from mine and scanned the park. She seemed close to tears. A firm handshake and empathy so strong that she was near tears in the middle of a public park. Beth Lind was an enigma.

"Thank you. It's been several years now, but I

appreciate the sentiment." I had received condolences from distant family and acquaintances, but none as intimate—and, I believed, heartfelt—as the one I'd just received.

She clasped her hand around my arm and, once we'd resumed our stroll, said, "Tell me about your sister. If you'd like."

I liked that very much, so I did.

Abigail had been lovely. Younger than me, but wiser in many ways. She understood people and society much better than I ever had. She'd encouraged me to pursue my love of nature and drawing, just as I'd encouraged her pursuits as a writer. She'd become an accomplished poet before she became ill. I shared all of this with Beth.

"You seem just fine with people."

"With you, perhaps. You put me at ease."

A bright smile lit up her face. "I feel the same." Her smile dimmed. "In the spirit of full disclosure, I have to tell you I'm not from here—or now."

"You're not from now?" As I spoke, an odd feeling churned in my gut—and it wasn't doubt.

"I don't suppose you've heard of H.G. Wells?"

"You're a time traveler?" I kept my expression studiously bland.

"Well, no. I'm a woman who's having a dream that she's time-traveled." Except that explanation didn't seem to please her at all. "Can you just pretend that I'm from the future and not a crazy person? If you do, then I'll go on pretending that you're not a dream and we're having this conversation in real life."

I didn't embrace the reality she presented, but neither could I fully reject it. This was a woman who had vanished from my arms a few weeks earlier, defying all known laws of science. Perhaps the science of her time had advanced sufficiently to explain the events of that evening—or perhaps she was unhinged...and we had *shared* a delusion?

My heart spoke for me when I asked, "When are you from?"

Again, I was graced with her smile. "Over a hundred years in the future, if it's 1899."

One hundred years. *More* than one hundred years.

We walked together silently while I digested the possibility that the woman by my side lived in a time that would be incomprehensible to me.

"Since you seem as confounded by our meeting as I, I infer that time travel is not commonly performed in the twenty-first century."

"No, only in fiction."

Her reference to H.G. Wells made good sense, then. I considered other fantastic futuristic works, then asked, "Travel to the moon?"

"Oh, yes, that one has happened."

I nodded as we began our second turn of the park. "Tell me of your time."

And she did.

That women dressed very differently, more for comfort and the weather rather than the time of day or social commitment, but also wearing what sounded like torturously uncomfortable footwear. Beth only agreed in part. It seemed she had a particular fondness for a shoe called a wedge but found stilettos as uncomfortable as they sounded.

She described a time when the freedoms were greater, as were the burdens. Her life sounded complicated in comparison to my own, but she seemed happy. And independent. Women attended university and held the same jobs as men.

Abigail would have loved this future Beth described.

"My sister believed education would change the future for women."

"She was right. Not only education, but that played a vital role." Beth hugged me closer to her side. "I'm sorry she'll never see those changes."

As was I. But something wonderful happened as I spoke of my sister: I felt Abigail's loss less keenly. It occurred to me that I'd missed this part of grieving, sharing the best moments, the brightest memories of Abigail with another person.

As we rounded a turn in the path, I leaned closer

to Beth—perhaps to tell her how much I had needed to speak of my sister, perhaps to thank her for the pleasure of her company—but she was gone.

Beth had disappeared with no warning.

Again.

5

BETH

I woke with a sense of dread in my belly.

Staring at the white, textured paint of my ceiling, it took me several disoriented seconds to pinpoint the cause: Edward's absence.

Waking in my own bed (not in a park), in an ice-blue chemise (not a rust-colored Victorian dress), and missing a man who wasn't real—that was the source of my distress.

I shouldn't have been experiencing emotions related to Edward, a man who existed only in my dreams.

Except...

A dream man wasn't supposed to give me a case of the feels, especially the sad feels.

He wasn't supposed to have parents and a sister who'd died.

Or bond with me over the oddities of twenty-first-century footwear.

Dream men were supposed to provide orgasms and cater to my every kinky need.

In all of those ways, my dreams had failed to hit the mark, and Hillary would definitely say my dreams sucked.

I disagreed, hence my downer mood. Waking up to the realization that all the feels and the fuzzies I'd experienced had been the result of my subconscious processing a miscellany of stored thoughts? Yeah, that sucked the big one.

No matter how vivid my memories seemed, the man I'd met was nothing more than a dream.

Ugh. My head was in a strange place. I grabbed my cell from my nightstand and came within a tap of calling Hillary. But then my alarm sounded, bringing with it reminders of my real life. Work waited for me, and I simply didn't have time in my schedule to mull over feelings I shouldn't have for a man who didn't exist.

One cancelled meeting later, as well as a finished project and a second project coming in ahead of schedule, and I was still telling myself I didn't have time to think about silly dreams. No time at all... even though I was now two days ahead of schedule.

When you lied to yourself, it wasn't really lying —was it?

I kept a lid on my Edward obsession until my head hit my pillow. But then I caved, grabbed my phone, and sent a text.

Have I told you about the weird dreams I've been having?

And then I waited. I knew I was poking a sex-on-the-brain bear, and I knew she'd be calling me right about—

My phone rang.

She didn't even let me say hello. "I want all the details."

"You perv." But I couldn't help laughing. I hadn't expected any less.

"Well, yeah, it's been a while for me. Holy bananas. It really has been a while. Almost a year since the last guy, what's-his-name."

Bananas? Was that sublimation? Not that bananas were all that phallic, but they kinda were? I snorted. "What's-his-name? You mean your ex-boyfriend? And you wonder why it didn't last."

"Sean, that was his name." But Hills had struggled to pull poor Sean's name from the depths of her memory. It seemed he wasn't all that memorable.

"Should I pat you on the back that you remember the name of the man you dated for four months?" I grabbed a packet of rice cakes from my nightstand drawer. *Yum, wasabi.*

"Please tell me you're not eating rice cakes."

"Okay, I won't. Anyhoo, my dream—which was not pervy, thank you very much—was completely weird."

"Much as I want to hear about your dream, I'd much rather hear about the Pringles you're eating." She paused, then said, "Sorry, the Cheetos. Or maybe the Funyuns?"

"Funyuns, Hills? Do you seriously eat those? Does anyone eat those?" I was poking fun, because anyone who knew Hillary knew she had a thing for Funyuns. Maybe that had been the real downfall of Sean and Hillary.

"You don't? What's wrong with you?"

Poor Hills. She'd been trying to eat healthier recently. Something to do with increasing her productivity. Not that I was one to downplay the benefits of a healthy diet, but there was such a thing as stages to improved eating. Hillary was going to go nutty on any kind of carb-free kick.

"I'm not answering that. Also, have a few Cheetos before you lose your mind. A few more days on a healthy diet and your system will be so shocked that you'll start seeing Brad."

Hill's resulting groan sounded tortured. Yeah, Brad would make anyone groan; I shouldn't have mentioned him. If my granddad were still alive and hallucinating a roommate named Brad (however helpful he might be), I'd be pretty worried, too.

"I can't find anything online about a Brad-type imaginary friend. Everything I've seen is really sad and deals with seniors who have a host of other problems. Gramps just had a physical about four months ago, and he's fit, thinks clearly, and seems completely fine. And trust me, I was very involved in the process and talked to his doctor. He's doing great."

"He's doing great, minus the guy who gives him advice and keeps him company. The one who isn't really there." I was sympathetic—I was—but Hillary needed to see the light and get her grandfather some help.

"Yep, minus that." She groaned again. "Brad stopped walking with him, because he didn't want people to see Gramps talking to himself, so, get this: Brad hooked him up with an audiobook app on his phone. Gramps is all excited about walking again."

"Man, that stinks. Brad sounds like a really nice guy."

"Right? But you don't know the worst of it. Aunt Carol and Uncle Tim have scheduled a psych eval."

"What?" I hollered. There was getting help and there was declaring your family member incompetent. Yikes. Softening my voice, I said, "Honey, I'm so sorry. They really want him out of that house, don't they?"

"It's so weird. Neither of them is hurting for cash,

and they swear they have his best interests at heart, but..."

"You're not so sure you believe them."

"If they bothered to spend more time with him, I might. Or if they trusted my opinion, as the person who spends the *most* time with him, I might."

"Uh..." I cleared my throat delicately. "The most outside of Brad."

"Not helping."

"No, what's not helping is how many hours you work. Get rid of your dog-walking business." I shushed her when she tried to interrupt. "Or your blogging gig. Something's gonna give."

"I'm working on it."

"Uh-huh. I'll believe it when you sound like you mean it. But for now, get a good night's sleep. Everything will look better in the morning."

And we ended the call on that note, my opportunity to discuss my odd, much-too-real dreams missed.

Not that it was weird that I could remember in excruciating detail what it felt like to walk in a tightened corset and skirts that almost dragged the ground. Not weird at all.

I couldn't burden my friend with a few silly, unexplainable dreams when she was facing her grandfather's possible eviction from his home and transfer to some institution for the mentally incompetent.

Walter was a really great guy. If you took the best grandpa ever, made him a little nicer, a little cuter, and just a tad eccentric, that would be Walter. His only faults were his terrible sense of style and his inability to see the bad in anyone, including his scheming kids.

I fluffed my pillow and slid back under my covers.

There was nothing else to do but go to bed.

To sleep.

To dream.

6

BETH

Clouds scattered across an otherwise blue sky, a gentle breeze ruffled my hair, and the leafed branches of a large tree shaded me from direct sunlight.

The first clue to my circumstances was the snug feeling of material around my neck, which I determined, after a brief investigation, to be a high neckline made of lace.

My twenty-first-century clothes didn't cover me to the chin, or cinch at the waist to then drape beautifully in a flow of floral fabric. The silk material of the gown I wore likely cost more than a few months' rent on my apartment, but it made the dress so pretty. Fragile, floating, edged in lace. Pretty was such a bland word, but this dress was absolutely pretty and not at all bland.

My modern clothes were affordable, comfortable, and flattering, but they didn't contain even a hint of the style and elegance of the clothing I wore in my dreams. My subconscious had excellent taste. Who knew? Hillary would be proud.

I was diverted from thoughts of fashion and time travel by the bearded man only a few feet away who appeared to be picnicking.

A bearded man I recognized immediately, even though his appearance was greatly altered. "Edward?"

He rose to his feet but didn't speak. He looked grim, perhaps a little tired.

I reached out a hand, mostly because I couldn't help myself. I needed to touch him.

Which was silly. I didn't even *know* him. And it wasn't as if the feel of his hand clasped in mine would prove his existence. The man was a dream. A figment of my imagination. A person made up by my subconscious to...what? To make me feel even worse about my lack of love life in the real world of the twenty-first century?

Whatever function his fictional existence served, my brain had decided that touch and smell were a part of the package. His hand was warm, his scent a now-familiar blend of woodsy, spicy man.

"Pinch me." I didn't really mean it when I said it,

but then I thought, why not? It wasn't like I'd wake up with a bruise.

"No." Edward's voice was rough. He cleared his throat and repeated his refusal. "Where have you been?"

I closed the gap between us, then reached out and ran my hand along his jaw, because this was my dream and I could. His beard wasn't long, maybe half an inch, but it was thick and surprisingly soft. "How...?"

"It's been more than a month since we last met." He tipped his head, leaning slightly into my touch.

Over a month? That was...odd. Why would time in my dreams pass differently than in my own life? My brain was a complicated place.

I met Edward's intent gaze. He had blue-green eyes and laugh lines around the corners. I hadn't considered his age before, but I'd guess he was a little older than me. Maybe early thirties. He definitely looked tired.

"Will you join me for a small meal, or would you prefer to walk?"

I looked around, beyond the shady tree, and found that we were completely alone. This grassy stretch was no city park. We were in the country.

From the meal laid out on a thin blanket, it looked like I'd interrupted his lunch.

There was a satchel nearby, large enough for the food I could see, the blanket, and a sketch pad. And there wasn't a carriage or horse in sight. It seemed Edward was on a nature walk. He'd told me during my last visit that he didn't get to explore and walk in the countryside as often now that he lived in town full time.

During my last visit...

This wasn't a *visit*. It was a dream. A vivid, fresh-grass-smelling dream.

But we'd agreed to disregard the inconsistencies of our meetings. Edward wouldn't think I was completely gaga when I talked about the future, and I would act as if he was a real, live man.

Dream Beth was breaking that agreement. I always lived up to my promises, and that should certainly hold true in a fantasy *I'd* concocted. Also, I was being rude. The poor man had been walking who knew how far and was probably hungry.

"I'll keep you company while you eat." I gave Edward's picnic blanket a critical look. My gauzy floral gown might make me feel pretty, but it sure as heck wasn't sensible. How was I supposed to sink gracefully to the ground in this getup?

Edward grinned. Gone was the serious man of mere moments earlier. "I can either turn my back or provide you with a steadying hand." He extended his gloveless hand and waited for my response.

At which point I dithered.

Flash an unseemly (by Victorian standards) amount of leg, or gracelessly fall to the ground while clutching the hand of a handsome gentleman?

Seriously, though, what red-blooded woman dreamt up a hottie then plopped him into one of the stuffiest time periods in recent history? My subconscious had a ridiculous sense of humor.

That was me: complicated and contrary, even while I slept.

From what I'd seen of Edward, the man didn't have a judgmental bone in his body, so I hitched up my skirts.

"Thanks, but I think I can manage." And then I dropped down on the blanket with all the grace of a...a...well, of a twenty-first-century woman decked out in ridiculously impractical clothing.

Edward refrained from commenting, following my lead instead. He was much more graceful as he stretched out his long legs.

Then again, he was wearing pants.

"I miss my pants," I said. Edward barked out a laugh, and I grinned back. "I don't suppose proper Victorian ladies covet men's trousers."

His grin reappeared. "I'm sure many do, but few discuss it in mixed company."

"You'd be shocked to hear what's considered normal conversation in my time."

"Unlikely." He held my gaze, but his scrutiny

didn't fluster me. I felt seen, appreciated. It was a pleasant change from my typical interactions with men. The flesh-and-blood, non-imaginary kind. Those kind of men—the real kind, especially if they looked even ten percent as attractive as Edward—made me blush and sweat and basically lose the ability to form coherent sentences.

When his gaze didn't falter after several seconds, I indicated his waiting meal. "Aren't you going to eat?"

He hesitated. "You're sure you won't join me?"

I shook my head.

In between bites, he told me about his trip to the country. He was staying at an inn and had spent the last few days walking and sketching. "I'm surprised you found me so far in the countryside."

"But I didn't. Find you, I mean. I went to bed, fell asleep, and here I am." I tugged at the high neckline of my gown. "Dressed like this."

His lips quirked, and I belatedly remembered our agreement to suspend disbelief. His smile broadened. "Perhaps we can assume an alternative explanation. A less practical one. A less skeptical one."

"Are we talking about God?" Because that seemed a little ridiculous. Why would the big guy worry himself with my dreams?

Apparently, Edward agreed, because he threw his head back and laughed. After a few mirth-filled seconds, he shook his head. "I was thinking more along the lines of the fantastic, not the heavenly."

"Oh." I frowned as I tried to recall any knowledge of magic in the early 1900s. Something about ghosts being a big thing, but nothing on time travel. "No, I'm not sure I follow."

"Perhaps a benevolent fairy has taken pity upon our plight." Something in my expression must have tipped him off that fairies weren't something I put much stock in. "You don't have fairies in the twenty-first century?"

"Yes?" But I was fairly certain he didn't mean the Disney variety, so I quickly amended my response. "Maybe. Wait, what do you mean 'our plight'?"

He didn't respond.

Not with words.

Instead, he leaned forward and kissed me.

Softly, gently, but with an intimacy I would never have expected from such a chaste, closed-mouth kiss.

Maybe it was the feel of his hand cupping my jaw.

Or the look in his eyes as he'd leaned closer.

As his lips firmed and my breath caught, I decided I didn't care about the why, because I just wanted more of Edward. More of his lips on mine. More of his hand touching my face. More—

I blinked blurry eyes at the textured ceiling in my bedroom. My twenty-first-century bedroom.

What followed wasn't my finest moment.

After a string of profanity and some serious pillow thumping, I tried desperately to go back to sleep.

When that failed, I gave myself a pep talk. It was just a dream. Edward was a figment of my overactive—and apparently very lonely—subconscious. I wasn't attracted to a man who didn't actually exist.

I wasn't falling for a man who wasn't real.

But I was, which was why I covered my face with my pillow and screamed like a toddler having a fit.

Not my finest moment.

7

EDWARD

I would never know how far that kiss would have gone.

My first kiss.

Not my actual first kiss—I was thirty-two; I'd had lovers—but the first kiss that mattered. The first kiss I'd felt to my core. The first kiss that had warmed places inside myself that I kept separate and private from the world.

And for all its innocence, it had also stirred me physically. Beth was an attractive woman. Her person, her personality, her intellect.

For the first time in my life, I saw a glimmer of something I'd never imagined. I'd pressed my lips to a woman's and wanted the feeling to last...forever.

If I had found my forever woman, if Beth was my One, then Fate was truly fickle.

First my parents were taken from me too young, then my great-aunt, and finally my sister. And now, Fate taunted me with glimpses of what could be.

I'd found a beautiful woman who made me smile, laugh, whose company I enjoyed so much that I craved her presence when she was absent. I missed her when she was gone, sought her out even though I knew she was unlikely to be found.

This time, I wouldn't seek her. This time, I'd have faith that she would come.

And when she did, I'd hang on for as long as Fate, that fickle wench, would let me have her.

When I was a child, my great-aunt Celia had told me stories of her world-traveling adventures. She'd been considered an eccentric. A widowed woman of means who went wherever her heart desired, even when it led her to the wilds of Africa.

She'd told me that someday I'd have my own adventures, that they might not involve crossing oceans or riding camels, that they would be *my* adventures, special and unique to me.

She'd told me to embrace my adventure when I found it.

Great-Aunt Celia was absolutely right. I'd found the adventure of a lifetime and her name was Beth.

I wasn't about to let go.

8

BETH

"I have news." Hills' calls came at strange times of the day, not at night. Usually she was juggling clients like mad, so I only heard from her in the evenings.

My laptop display said it was twelve fifteen. I'd made it out of bed this morning, reluctantly and later than usual by a good hour, but I'd made it. What hadn't accompanied me was my good humor. That had been left in a prematurely terminated dream alongside a kissable Victorian gentleman.

Why was Hillary calling me at midday? That's right: she had news.

Since she was waiting for me to reply before dropping some kind of truth bomb, I decided to take a wild guess. "Don't tell me. You've sold all four of your businesses, and you're moving to Alaska."

Silence followed.

"Hills?"

"Close."

"What's close? Wait, you're moving to Alaska?" A panicky fluttering started in my chest. Hillary and I didn't see nearly enough of each other, but she was my best friend in the world.

She snorted. "Please. Me? In Alaska?"

A smile tugged at my lips. Now that I knew she wasn't ditching me for the far north, I could let myself linger over visions of Hillary in her high heels and impractical clothes in Alaska. "I hear there are lots of rugged, single men up there."

"Yeah, about that. I'm dating someone."

That was new. Hillary went out with men. Met up with them. Hung out, did drinks or dinner, basically anything and everything but "dating." She had an aversion to the word. She'd been dating her last boyfriend for three months before she even called it dating, and then they broke up a month later.

Maybe—miracle of miracles—Hillary was finally falling in *love* and not just *lust*. "Who? Do I know him? Did you meet him at work? What was your first date? *When* was your first date?"

Rather than a rush of answers—which was what I'd expected—she hemmed and hawed for a few seconds and finally said, "His name is Brad."

"No way! You are not dating a guy with the same name as your grandad's imaginary friend."

"No, I'm not dating a guy with the same name. I'm dating the guy. I'm dating Brad."

Thankfully, a knock at my door saved me from saying anything I'd regret, like "Have you lost your ever-loving mind?" As I made my way to the front door, I considered how many people visited me at my apartment. Three, and two of them didn't live in town.

"Are you at my front door?"

"Uh-huh. And I brought Brad with me."

My hand hovered over the doorknob.

Worst case, she'd caught her grandfather's hallucination (and yes, I was well aware hallucinations weren't contagious) and was alone.

Second worst case, her sense of humor had taken a nosedive and landed in the realm of tasteless and terrible.

Third worst case—no, bump that up to *worst* worst case—there was actually a guy named Brad waiting on the other side of that door.

"Beth? Open the dang door. I'm not a lunatic, promise, and I haven't been replaced by a pod person."

Pod people hadn't even made my list. Sheesh, where was my mind these days? Oh, yeah, hung up on a guy who lived in my head and nowhere else.

I swung open the door to find Hills and a very tall, very attractive man on the other side. A little too pretty for my taste, but Hillary didn't seem to think so, given the besotted look on her face.

And Ms. I Hate PDA was in the hallway in front of my apartment holding hands with that pretty man. No, they weren't climbing on top of each other in the middle of the street, but Hillary had never been a hand-holding kind of girl.

Hillary glanced at her clasped hand, blushed (Hills never blushed!), and quickly let go. My best friend, who talked about sex like most people would their laundry or doing dishes, was blushing over a little hand-holding.

Dang it. Now I wanted to like the fraud standing on my doorstep. The one claiming to be Brad, a guy who didn't exist.

Speaking of guys who didn't exist and the women who had feelings for them... Warning bells dinged in my head, but I ignored them. This was about Brad, not Edward.

Brad extended his hand. "It's a pleasure to meet you. I've heard so much about you, I almost feel like we've met before."

I shook his hand but didn't reply. Mostly because I hadn't a clue what to say. "You're a fraud" seemed like the entirely wrong way to start. And "Are you delusional as well?" didn't seem too sharp either.

As I stood gaping, Hillary pushed past me and tugged fake Brad behind her.

Once we were all in the kitchen, Hillary started to speak, but Brad stopped her with a hand on her back. "Maybe coffee or tea first? It's kind of a long story."

So I made tea—herbal; no way was I adding caffeine to the mix—while Hillary spun a fantastic tale. One with a wicked almost-mother-in-law (Brad's), a curse (also Brad's), and a fairy godmother (Hillary's).

When she got to the end, the part about her grandfather, I couldn't help but interject. "Wait, are you saying that your aunt and uncle are done hassling Walter? He can stay in his house? They don't want to kick him to the curb?"

Brad frowned. "They weren't trying to make him homeless. Just move him."

I arched an eyebrow and gave him my hairy eyeball look. "Move him to a facility for seniors with declining cognitive function."

He shrugged. "They love him. They were just confused. Since they've been coming over for dinner more often, they're a lot more comfortable with Walter staying in the house."

Hillary leaned into Brad, and he wrapped an arm around her. "It doesn't hurt that you're his roommate." She grinned up at him. "They really like you."

Brad—the imposter fraudster—hugged my bestie against his side. "Thanks, hon. I'm glad."

I'd think they were sweet if Brad wasn't a charlatan and—oh, yeah—if they both hadn't lost their ever-loving minds.

"You both know there is no such thing as fairy godmothers? And that you sound like complete lunatics."

Hillary bit her lip. "Yeah, I get that it sounds nuts, but if you'd seen all the things we had, you'd believe." Hillary gave me a pleading look. "I could have gone with a version of the truth—that Brad was this great guy I'd met and that he and Gramps were now roomies, and it was just a coincidence that he shared a name with Gramps's imaginary friend—but I needed you to know everything. Even the scary magic parts."

Scary magic parts. I crossed my arms. Hillary had a psychic who read auras. *She* didn't think magic was scary. I, on the other hand, was a nonbeliever, because if magic was real, that was scary.

If magic was real…? Seriously?

Except I was having really weird, unexplainable —not scary—dreams.

But dreams weren't magic.

The "buts" and "what-ifs" and "excepts" tangled around inside my head, and my mind started to flash danger signals like crazy.

Maybe I should tell Hillary about the dreams. *What? Bad brain. Shame on you.* No way was I having that conversation with "I believe I'm dating imaginary Brad" Hillary. That version of Hillary wasn't up for it. Or maybe I wasn't up for what that version of Hillary had to say.

"What was that? That look." Hillary squinted, giving me her version of a hairy eyeball (except hers was about two percent as effective as mine).

"I have no idea what you mean." I was not talking about weird, too-real dreams with bright colors and vivid scents and one very hot Victorian man.

Her eyes narrowed further, then she turned to Brad. "Honey, can you go pick up some lunch for us?"

Brad's gaze slipped from Hillary to me and back again. "Sandwiches and chips?" Then he named Hillary's favorite deli and asked if she wanted the usual.

A small pang of envy made me swallow. I wanted that for her. She deserved a man who knew her favorite sandwich shop. Someone who could read her need for privacy in a flash and acted without hesitation. Someone who remembered her ridiculous love of meatball sandwiches and then told her he wouldn't forget the Funyuns.

She must have the best breath mints ever. Supercharged breath mints. *Magic* breath mints.

I wanted all of that for her, even the Funyuns and the supercharged breath mints. But I also wanted that for myself—minus the disgusting food.

Once I'd added my order and Brad had shut the door behind him, she turned to me and said, "Spill."

"Seriously? You show up with a boyfriend and then tell me this crazy story, and you expect us to talk about some imagined drama in *my* life."

Deflection usually had a ten to twenty percent chance of success with Hillary, but luck was not on my side today.

"All true statements, and yes I do." Hands on hips, she repeated, "Spill."

If we'd been on the phone, I'd have ended the call, but with her here, in my kitchen, staring at me... I caved. And this was why she could never learn of my love of sparkly things. Hillary was my kryptonite.

"I'm having weird dreams."

She frowned. "Still? Didn't you tell me, like, a month ago that you were having weird dreams?"

Had it been a month? I hadn't had a dream every night. And time for Edward had moved much faster than it had for me, but... "I guess? I'm not sure. I don't have them every night."

"But when you do, they're really weird." She waggled her eyebrows in what was supposed to be a suggestive manner, but just looked ridiculous.

"Hills, they're not sex dreams."

She pursed her lips. "Too bad. It's not like you're getting any in real life. Might as well live it up in your subconscious."

She wasn't wrong. Not entirely. But instead of living up to my lack of sex life while I slept, I was developing real feelings for a guy who only existed in my head.

The parallels to Hillary's situation weren't lost on me, but since I didn't believe her cockamamie fairy godmother story, I sure as heck didn't think anything could come of my imaginary guy.

"What's percolating in that head of yours?" After yet another squinty-eyed look, she headed for the fridge. Two seconds of peering at the interior and she sighed. "Skinny margarita mix? Even when you're unhealthy, you're healthy. That's just wrong, Beth. So wrong."

But that didn't stop her from making two margaritas.

There was no use in arguing when she was like this. She had a driver, and I was hardly having a productive day anyway, so why not?

She plopped two salt-rimmed glasses down on the kitchen table and pointed to a chair. "Sit."

I sat.

Once she'd taken the chair kitty-corner, I stalled by taking a sip of my drink. But Hillary knew my sneaky ways. She waited until the weight of the silence was too much for me and I cracked. "His name is Edward."

She whooped, then did a fist pump. "I knew there was a man. What does he look like? Tall, short, facial hair? No man-bun, right? That wouldn't work for a Victorian guy. But those Victorians loved their facial hair. Spill. Oh! Build—skinny, muscular? Now spill."

Why not? The distraction from the bigger issue —me having feelings for an imaginary man— wouldn't hurt. "Definitely clean-shaven. Taller than me, maybe half a foot taller? Broad shoulders. I'm not sure about build, Hill. He was wearing a suit."

No need to delve into the arm-porn arena with Hillary. And that was yet more proof of his imaginary state. What Victorian gentleman would be as buff as Edward?

"A suit, huh? Fair enough. Benedict Cumberbatch, Ryan Reynolds, or Channing Tatum?"

"Oh, um, Ryan Reynolds, I guess?"

"Way to score a hottie. I knew you had it in you, sweetie. You just needed a little push."

"There's no scoring, because there is no man. That's the issue. I'm having these dreams." I pointed a finger at her and leveled her with a shush look before she could make a sex joke. "Not about sex. About... I don't know, Hills. About dating?"

I winced, waiting for the wisecracks to start.

But they never came, which was why Hillary was my best friend.

She grasped my hand and squeezed my fingers. "Are you falling in love with this man from your dreams? With Edward?"

And that was when I bawled. I wasn't a crier, but what woman was pathetic enough to fall for a man who didn't even exist?

Hillary pulled a packet of tissues from her purse and offered me one. Then she rubbed my back and waited. When my brief storm of self-pitying tears had passed, she said, "I think you need to meet Madeleine."

"Who?"

"My fairy godmother."

I dabbed at my eyes and then swallowed another sip of margarita. The tang of the salt and citrus on my tongue was comforting. I could barely taste the tequila, so I was pretty sure Hillary had only added a tiny splash of alcohol. "You want me to meet your fairy godmother, who happens to be named Madeleine?"

"I do. Hear me out." She leaned forward with an earnest expression, so I listened. "You're practical. I mean, super practical. You don't do weird dreams. You're also crazy shy, or you'd be married three times over."

"What?" I didn't get the logic there at all.

"You want to be in a stable relationship, but you won't date just to date—he has to be the right guy. You'd never compromise. You'd only date someone you really cared about, but you never get to know men well enough to care about them because you're so shy. You see where I'm going with this?"

She wasn't wrong, but I hadn't a clue where she was going with this. "Yeah, not at all."

"You're falling in love with a guy who isn't real—your dream man Edward—because you're not shy around him and you're actually getting to know him, and he's awesome."

I snorted. "Of course he's awesome. My subconscious made him awesome. *He's not real.*"

"What if that's not the case? What if he's a real guy? What if *you* have a fairy godmother? What if you've been set up in one of the only ways you could be, because you're so crazy shy when it comes to men and romance. Which, by the way, I do not understand, because you're insanely hot." She blinked innocent eyes at me. "I'd totally do you if I was into women—well, into women and not dating Brad, which I wouldn't be, because I'd be into women."

I grinned, because it wasn't the first time she'd told me that. "You know I'm not really a 'do you' kind of girl. I'm more a wine-me, dine-me, meet-my-parents kind of girl."

"Yeah, yeah. Whatever. You get my point. You're falling in love, and that's a minor miracle in itself. Does the how really matter?"

"Yes, Hillary. Yes, it matters, because I'm falling in love with a man who doesn't exist. That is heartache wrapped up in a straitjacket."

"Pshaw. He exists. You could never fall in love with some two-dimensional fake guy. I don't know who this Edward guy is—"

"Stanbury. His name is Edward Stanbury."

"Beth! No one has dreams of guys with last names. This guy is real."

"And smells great," I mumbled.

"Holy banana split sundaes. Are you kidding me? Dreams definitely don't come with smells. Not usually, anyway. I mean, I guess it's possible? But I'm going with this guy being a real dude somewhere. We just have to find him."

That was insane, and I told her so. "Oh, also, he's Victorian."

I waited to see how she could explain that one away, but she just looked at me.

"I don't get it. Victorian what? Like he lives in a great big house that has old plumbing?"

"No. He lives in London…in 1899."

She blinked. Three times. And just when I

thought I'd stumped her, she got that squinty look in her eyes again. "Oh, you are definitely meeting Madeleine. I smell sparkly fairy dust all over this."

"Please, with the fairy godmother stuff again. Auras are bad enough, but really, Hillary, a fairy godmother?"

She tipped her head to the side. "Actually, she prefers FG. She feels like fairy godmothers have a branding issue."

"You're missing the point. Also, sparkle dust doesn't smell."

Which was just idiotic. If there were such a thing as fairy godmother sparkle dust, for all I knew, it smelled like sunshine and unicorns and lollipops.

Hillary arched an eyebrow. "As soon as Brad gets here, we'll hit him up to drive us to Every Woman's Fairy Godmother. He'll have eaten at the deli to give us more time, so we can make him drive while we eat on the way."

Because we couldn't skip a meal. Not in Hillary's world. Or eat peacefully at the kitchen table and then go to...

"Uh, where are we going?"

She grinned, then downed her drink. "Every Woman's Fairy Godmother. You'll love it."

No, I wouldn't. It sounded woo-woo and magicky and kitschy and like something I would absolutely *not* like.

9
BETH

"They're so pretty." I couldn't peel my eyes away from the display cases of vintage jewelry. Some of it was costume, some real, but all of it was *so pretty*.

"Beth?"

Hillary had left me at the front door to find Madeleine, her supposed fairy godmother.

I traced my finger along the glass near a particularly fine cocktail ring. Too big for me, but I could admire it from afar. "Hm?"

"Beth!"

With a guilty start, I looked up.

She must have come up empty-handed, because she was alone. "You sneaky, skinny blonde girl. How have you kept *that* a secret for so long?"

Hills always called me skinny blonde girl when

she was trying to push my buttons. I *was* thin and blonde, and I wasn't particularly sensitive about either—but that was Hills, and she was letting me know I'd been found out.

Busted.

I considered my options and went with the only reasonable choice: deny, deny, deny. "I don't know what you're talking about."

But then my traitorous eyes slipped to the right, and I spotted the last thing I'd thought I'd ever see in real life: a gorgeous sapphire necklace identical in design to the bracelet I'd worn in the first dream I'd had of Edward.

Beth was chattering in my ear, but I didn't comprehend a word. That necklace pulled me closer, and all I could think as I approached was *how?*

I'd never been to this store. I'd never seen this necklace. Why—how—did a vintage store even have such a fine piece? It had to be worth a small fortune.

"It's beautiful, isn't it?" The whispered words finally caught my attention, and they weren't spoken by Hillary. An attractive brunette stood next to me, her gaze on the necklace. "It's a matching set, but the bracelet's been temporarily separated from its mate."

No. Uh-uh. No way.

I must have actually said that out loud and not just in my head, because she replied, "Oh yes. But don't worry. It's safe for now." Then she grinned, and a dimple popped up in her right cheek.

She'd be adorable, if I didn't feel like she'd just crawled inside my head and taken a long, hard look at all my crazy.

Because the ideas in my head weren't what anyone would call rational.

Edward was *not* real.

The bracelet was *not* real.

Edward did not currently have possession of the bracelet that matched the necklace right in front of me.

A necklace that existed in the twenty-first century.

A necklace with a matching bracelet that was lost in the late nineteenth century.

"It's not lost. Your gentleman has it safely locked away, waiting for an opportunity to return it."

I must have been babbling my random and completely impossible thoughts. I stared at her, then at Hills, who stood next to her looking more than a little worried.

When my bestie met my gaze, she faked a reassuring smile. "Beth, this is Madeleine. Madeleine, this is—"

"Beth Lind." Madeleine extended her hand. After I'd shaken it, she said, "I'm quite familiar with her. She's a client."

"Um, no." Denial seemed the order of the day, so I went with it. "I don't think so."

"We haven't met in person, but I've been working on your case."

"My case?" She sounded like a social worker. I didn't need anyone working on "my case." And without consulting me? That was wrong on so many levels. "I didn't hire you. You can't do that."

I looked at Hillary for backup, except that was a mistake, because Hillary was among the newly converted. She was dating Brad, Mr. Imaginary Friend, who, actually, was turning out to be a gem, whoever he really was. He'd dropped us off at the door and told Hillary that he was going to work at a coffee shop a few doors down until we were ready to go. The man knew how to be there for his lady and when to quietly disappear.

Hillary shrugged. "It's her FG talent. Madeleine knows your deepest wish. Your heart's true desire. And it's not like it's any huge secret. I've known since sixth grade that you were a white-picket-fence, golden-retriever, two-point-four-kids kinda girl. I'm pretty sure y*ou've* known that on some level since the fifth grade. But then you dated a few losers, and now you're not dating at all."

That was completely unfair. I dated.

Sort of.

Okay, I thought about dating, it just didn't happen.

And I wasn't into golden retrievers and white picket fences. It was like she didn't know me at all.

Maybe a little terrier mix with a nice privacy fence in the back so my cute little dog didn't get his head stuck or bark at the neighbors when I let him out.

Oh. My. God.

Who was I kidding? Hillary was right.

But that didn't mean they hadn't both lost their minds. Time for a reality check. I shifted so I couldn't catch the necklace out of the corner of my eye and addressed Madeleine.

"You're not a fairy godmother, because those aren't real." I turned to Hillary and said, "And you're not dating Walter's Brad, because he's not real." I paused then added, "But whoever he is, he seems very nice."

Hillary's lips twitched. "Uh-huh. He is."

"I don't believe any of this whackadoo stuff you're both spouting," I said to Madeleine. And yet I had questions, so... "But just for argument's sake, if any of this were true—which is impossible, but if it were—why would you ever set me up with a long-distance relationship?"

"A really, really long-distance relationship," Hills

muttered. "Oh, hey! Why didn't she have to wear glasses?"

I'd forgotten about that part of Hillary's story. She hadn't seen Brad until she wore the supposed magic glasses, which had allowed her to see her one true love. I mean, could it be cheesier?

Said my rational mind.

Romantic me squealed with excitement and cheered in a high-pitched, girly voice. Romantic me was silly and shouldn't be allowed to see the light of day.

Madeleine looked uncomfortable, but then Hills elbowed her and said, "Come on. I'm your most successful client. You can tell me."

The two shared a look I couldn't quite interpret, then Madeleine said, "After your case, I decided props could be unpredictable, so this time I went with a more hands-on approach." Then her dimple returned as she grinned. "You and Brad inspired me. After seeing how happy you both are, I decided that I wouldn't let the little things get in the way of a great match."

Aww. Edward and I were a great match.

And that was romantic me. I needed to slap that girl silly. "Little things? Like over a hundred years of time and an ocean? No big deal."

Madeleine's grin just broadened. "Not at all, when it comes to love."

"I am not joining this crazy train. You're both delusional."

"You mean all three of us are." Hillary stood in front of the case containing the sapphire and diamond necklace and tapped her finger on the glass. "Your best friend since grade school, her boyfriend, and a respected business owner—all delusional. You're the only sane one of the three of us."

"See how easy that is to admit?" It was an automatic reply, because I didn't want to consider what Hills was saying.

I didn't want to consider that the foundation of the world in which I lived could be shifting. That was scary. I liked solid, nonmagical ground under my feet. Ground that was based on fact and physics and other sciencey things that I didn't completely understand but had faith in.

But...

Wasn't there a saying? Magic is science that has yet to be explained? Or something like that.

And...

If fairy godmothers existed—big if, huge if, monstrous if—but *if* they did, then maybe men in dreams could be real?

"Give her a second," Hills said to Madeleine. "The wheels are turning."

Which earned her a glare. "Don't make fun. I'm considering *your* highly improbable proposition."

Hillary patted Madeleine's arm. "She doesn't mean anything by it. It's just her process."

Madeleine clasped her hands together. "Oh, no. I'm not offended. This is fun. And she's right: magic is highly improbable. It's magic."

As if that explained everything. That explained nothing.

"Brad's doing well." Hillary changed the subject, and the two of them chatted about Brad and his mom and how she was adjusting to having her son rise from the dead. It seemed everyone had presumed Brad dead for the last several years, a suspected suicide, but his mom had refused to believe it.

My heart hurt for that poor woman. "Wow. I didn't know that part. I'm really sorry, Hills."

She flashed me a small smile. "It's okay. His mom is doing really well. It was a shock, for sure, but the best kind. All of her hopes were realized when he came back."

And in that moment, I believed. In Brad, in magic...in Edward.

Maybe it was the fact that not everything in Hillary and Brad's relationship was roses and sunshine (the man had practically disappeared from the face of the planet for a few years, leaving grieving friends and family behind), maybe Hillary was right and I'd just needed to process at my own speed, or maybe Madeleine had sprinkled a little fairy dust on me when I wasn't looking.

Maybe all three.

But I believed. Mostly. Sort of.

I hugged Hills hard. "I'm sorry you went through all of that alone."

Because it wasn't like she could have called up her best friend and said, "Hey, I'm falling in love with my grandfather's imaginary friend," and I'd have been supportive.

For most major life events, I was an excellent go-to gal. On the subject of all things woo-woo, we've always agreed to disagree.

"She wasn't alone. She had Brad and Walter and me," Madeleine said. And I didn't even feel like it was a rebuke. Or that my friendship with Hills had been impinged upon. No, just that Hillary's fairy godmother—her FG (and I couldn't help a smile at that thought)—had stepped in when she needed help.

I gave her a mild version of the hairy eyeball. "But really, setting her up with a cursed man?"

Hills bumped shoulders with me. "And setting *her* up with a guy from another time?"

"Yes, well, true love can be found in surprising

places." Madeleine spoke with confidence, but there was something...

My hairy eyeball turned hairier. "Edward is real, isn't he?"

"Yes!" She seemed startled by the question. "Of course he is. Very real, and the best possibility for your one true love that I could find."

When I about went cross-eyed sorting through how my *one* true love had multiple possibilities, Hillary jumped in. "Love evolves over time, so Madeleine finds the best possibility for the person who could become your true love." She looked at me and shrugged. "Just go with it."

Madeleine nodded, and yet she still seemed a little...hesitant.

"What's the problem?" I asked firmly, though I did turn down the evil-eyed stare a little. The woman was trying to find me my very own true love, after all. Romantic me and practical me were on the same page for that one. We both liked that idea very much.

"No problem." Except there wasn't quite as much conviction in her voice and demeanor as I would have liked.

"So how does this work, now that I'm in on the big secret? I mean, is the real-life Edward living in downtown Austin and working the theater circuit?"

Hills and Madeleine both looked a little uncomfortable. "He's really in London, isn't he?"

Madeleine nodded, then she and Hillary exchanged a look.

Well, hell. I knew what that meant. "And he's really in 1899. Still. Right now. Not just in my dreams."

"That's not exactly how time works. It's more fluid than..." Madeleine blinked at the return of my hairy eyeball. "Basically, yes."

"So how do we end up in the same place in real life?" I asked. Madeleine tipped her head without answering, which prompted my next, much more panicked, question. "We can end up in the same place in real life, right? This isn't supposed to be a long-distance-by-dream relationship, is it?"

Because that would be bad. Really bad. That would drive me around the bend. Falling in love with a man I only saw in my dreams—my unpredictably timed dreams—would be a nightmare.

"What? No! Of course you can be in the same place." When Hillary poked her with a sharp elbow, Madeleine quickly added, "And time. Absolutely."

"How exactly does that work?" Hillary sounded suspicious, and she was the one who was fully on board with magic and fairy godmother sparkle magic dust.

"I can't say," the shifty fairy replied. Shifty, shady,

highly suspect—not the way I'd describe fairy godmothers prior to my current encounter. Then again, I'd have said they were fictional before today.

"Can you get them in the same place?" Hills asked. "Because you know this whole love thing only works when they actually live in the same time zone, or time period. Whatever. You know what I mean. Can you do it?"

Ding, ding, ding, ding. Give my bestie a prize. I knew she had my back.

"I can't say." Madeleine avoided looking at me.

I swallowed a groan, because—really? She didn't *seem* like she wanted to ratchet up my stress to ulcer-inducing levels. And she had finagled Hillary into an introduction with the one man who could pierce her commitment-phobic heart.

Which led me to chew over her reply.

I. Can't. Say.

Very different from "I don't know if I can." Or "I don't know how."

Hillary was turning a delicate shade of pink, which could be the precursor to regrettable words. Before she could turn into a complete mama bear on my behalf, I said, "You think Edward and I have a real shot at a relationship."

Madeleine clapped her hands and hopped a little. "Yes!"

If I wasn't so peeved, I'd think it was adorable.

She looked a little like a well-dressed cheerleader, rooting for her favorite team. The heels and the dress weren't exactly standard issue for cheerleaders, but she had the bounce and the enthusiasm down pat. All of which confirmed my gut feeling that she was on Team Edward and Elizabeth.

I tried another approach. "You think Edward and I can be together."

She bounced and grinned. "Yes!"

"But you can't say more than that."

She nodded.

Hillary groaned. "Is this part of that whole 'and the little human peoples will not know of magic and fairies' schtick they try to make you follow?"

Madeleine wrinkled her nose.

"Seriously? We know you're a fairy godmother. Hasn't that ship sailed?"

She shrugged but also gave Hillary an apologetic look.

I wasn't ready to argue, because...magic.

And fairy godmothers.

And magic.

I was *not* a magic-believing kind of girl.

And yet...Brad and Hillary.

And the necklace that matched the bracelet.

And the weird feeling in my gut that my overly vivid dreams of Edward were too real not to *be* real.

"Let's go."

I must have looked as resolute as I felt, because Hillary didn't argue. "Yes, let's." She pointed at her own eyes with two fingers then Madeleine's with one. As if she could pull off a tough-guy "watching you" gesture. What little impact she might have made was erased by her next words. "Oh, and I forgot to tell you, Brad and Walter got a new grill. They want you to come by for hamburgers sometime."

I snorted.

"What? They do. That doesn't mean I don't have your back, lady. We'll figure this Edward thing out, even if a certain FG doesn't want to help us."

Madeleine waved cheerily as we exited the store, so I was pretty sure she wasn't feeling too remorseful about her failure to deliver the full skinny.

10

EDWARD

Whenever I left the house, I looked for Beth's familiar figure.

My mind began playing tricks on me.

I'd catch faint traces of the floral scent she wore, unique and quite possibly not to be created for another hundred years.

I'd spot a familiar curve of a jaw or tilt of a head.

I'd hear a laugh in the distance and hope that it might be her.

Weeks of this trickery passed and still she failed to appear.

I began to avoid what few social commitments remained on my calendar, instead turning my attention to the one activity that could hold my attention for more than a few minutes at a time: observing and documenting local flora and fauna.

The humid air smelled of cut grass and blooming roses. I'd chosen a public rose garden for my outing, because roses reminded me of Beth. I wasn't certain *why*. I had no knowledge of her favorite flower. I'd never had the privilege of sending her a bouquet. Never had a conversation in which she'd stated her preference of bloom. Didn't even know if she liked freshly cut flowers or preferred chocolates.

A light sprinkling of rain removed any chance of sketching, but since the overcast sky so perfectly matched my mood, I wasn't particularly disappointed.

I was developing feelings for a woman so far out of my reach that I couldn't begin to imagine how we might ever be in the same place. I pinched the bridge of my nose in an attempt to ward off a headache, because *place* wasn't the greatest obstacle.

My mind still stuttered over the implications of time travel, and in the darkest hour of my sleepless nights, I questioned my sanity. In the light of day, however, I had no such qualms. Beth's presence in my life was too real to be imagined.

She was vibrant. When we spoke, we understood one another in a way I hadn't experienced since I'd lost my sister. Beth and I connected in a way that reminded me of my relationships with Abigail and my great-aunt Celia, though my feelings for Beth couldn't be further from familial.

And now my thoughts wandered down a path best left untrod. Steering my mind to safer ground, I walked the paths of the rose garden and recalled my first meeting with Beth. She'd been stunning.

She was always stunning. Stunning, enchanting, thoughtful, intelligent, funny...

My breath caught in my chest. She was here. In the rose garden. With me.

A shaft of sunlight broke through the clouds and shone upon her golden hair, bringing to mind an angel. Had my imagination gone wild? Had I lost touch with reality?

The clouds parted, and the sun's warmth touched my skin. I inhaled the damp smells of the garden. Moist earth, greenery, and the floral scent of several rose varietals perfumed the air.

If this moment was one of my imagining, it was the most vibrant of hallucinations.

"Edward!" The words seemed to be startled from Beth's lips as she turned and saw me on the path.

Her fair skin flushed pink, and she stilled like a frightened deer a mere moment before fleeing.

I approached cautiously. "Beth, it's good to see you. More time has passed than ever before between your visits. I feared..."

The words faded away. Voicing my fears would only make them more tangible.

She nodded as though in agreement, but her expression lacked the warmth I'd grown accustomed to seeing. Any animation at all. She still appeared frozen.

After some consideration, I tucked her hand under my arm and continued in the direction she appeared to be walking before spotting me. Beth was uncomfortable, and while I wasn't certain for the reason, I'd do my best to put her at ease.

Several minutes of silence followed as Beth and I walked along the graveled path. Her slight form eventually relaxed, but I was forced to hold my tongue while we passed an elderly couple strolling in the same direction and a nanny with a pram traveling the opposite.

When we were again guaranteed privacy, I cleared my throat and indicated a hot-air balloon ascending in the distance. "I didn't think the weather would clear, but the clouds have blown past and the aeronauts are launching."

Beth smiled and my heart warmed. It was the first smile I'd received since her arrival.

"Have you ever ridden in one?" I asked.

"A hot-air balloon? No, I haven't." She stared at the brightly colored balloon now drifting in the air. "Have you?"

"I'd planned to, but...time got away from me." First my adventure-loving great-aunt's death, then the onset of my sister's illness, followed by her death. Without my great-aunt or Abigail, my life had lost its vibrancy.

Beth had brought the color back into my life. I hadn't truly appreciated that fact until this moment. I turned my head to admire a nearby rosebush filled with pale pink blooms. It was that or speak words Beth wasn't ready to hear.

Quietly, almost shyly, Beth said, "You should make time. Don't wait any longer."

I nodded, because she was right. Not necessarily about a balloon ride, but about my life. I'd been allowing my grief and solitude to guide my choices. I'd been waiting. Waiting for the sadness to pass. Waiting for life to entice me out of my melancholic state.

I nodded again. "You're right. I shouldn't wait."

Her fingers tightened on my arm, and then she was gone.

11

BETH

Cursing wasn't my go-to form of communication, but Hillary got an earful when I called her.

"Calm your butt down, lady." A few seconds later, she said, "Wait, do you know what time it is?"

No. No, I did not.

I woke up, remembered my dream that wasn't actually a dream but a whacked-out, time-traveling interaction with a guy I was a little nuts about, got terribly embarrassed by my freakish behavior, then called my bestie.

I pulled my phone away from my ear long enough to determine it was early.

Very early.

"Sorry, Hills."

"Yeah, okay." The sound of sheets rustling in the

background was followed by the quiet murmuring of a male voice.

Somebody was shacking up with a former ghost turned real-life hottie. "Say hi to Brad."

Hills snorted. "I will not. Brad is going back to sleep, because he has to be up in a bit to walk dogs."

I hadn't realized Brad was pitching in with Hillary's dog-walking business, but it made sense. She was overcommitted with her four businesses, and desperately needed the help.

I couldn't help a tiny "Aww."

"That's right: aww. Brad is the best, and he's even better when he gets enough sleep because then he's the best and not cranky. And since we were up late last night—"

"Stop there. I don't think I can handle sexual innuendo this early in the morning." Who was I kidding? It wasn't the hour, it was my lack of sex life that made hearing about Hills' sexy times so hard.

"No innuendo," Hills replied. "We had great sex. We always have great sex. And Brad is seriously hu—"

"Eh, eh, eh. Stop! No details. I have to look him in the face." And now I'd be thinking about parts of Brad I'd rather be ignorant of every time I saw him for the next few weeks. Thanks so much for that, Hillary. She knew how shy I was around good-looking guys—not that Brad counted, because he was Hillary's other half, but still. And speaking of being shy... I groaned.

"What happened?" Running water splashed in the background. Hillary was probably making coffee. "Tell me. You woke me up with the first f-bomb I've heard leave your mouth in years. Oh, no. Did something happen with Eddie?"

"Ew. Eddie? Please don't ever call him that. His name is Edward, Hills. Edward. As in dignified, but cute and also smart. And hot. And really sweet." I smacked the pillow next to me in bed. "He's no Eddie."

"Eddies the world over are telling you where you can go. My water is about to boil, which means my coffee is about to be made, which means you have about four minutes to spill before I'm hanging up and enjoying my morning caffeine in peace."

An empty threat. Hillary had some serious FOMO. She wanted all the Edward info, and she wasn't limiting me to a four-minute breakdown. That said, the story was pretty short. I could sum it up in one sentence.

"I was weird."

"That's not enough information, sweetie. Weird like that time you dressed up as Han Solo for Halloween? Or that time you were the witch who ate Hansel and Gretel for that festival thingy? By the way, cannibalism is not a good look on you. And the hairy wart didn't help."

I glared, but since she was miles away, that wasn't particularly helpful. "I was Han Solo for the festival thingy and the witch for Halloween." Both completely appropriate costumes for the occasions, thank you very much. And I rocked cannibalism when it was of the German fairy tale variety.

"Or weird like the time when Doug asked you out in the eighth grade and you cried and then laughed and then cried and then looked like you might puke?"

I squinted and glared some more. If she was here, I'd smack her. I couldn't believe she'd pulled out the Doug story. We'd agreed the Doug incident was never to be spoken of again. Also, I *did* puke—two minutes later, after Doug had run away terrified and I'd run to the girls' bathroom.

"Or weird like the time you—"

"Oh my gosh, will you stop already? You make me sound like a complete freak." I stopped, considered my last meeting with Edward, and then fell back against my pillow. I pulled my comforter over my head and said, "I am, aren't I? I'm a total freak."

My voice was muffled, but I was pretty sure Hillary could still understand me, and I needed to hide under the covers right now. I needed to hide from myself and my embarrassment.

Hills sighed. "You're not. You do have an odd love of ridiculous, not-at-all-sexy costumes, and a bizarre fear of processed food. And you do talk about retirement more than any other person I've ever met under the age of fifty—but you're endearing and charming and lovable. Heck, you're even likable. Honey, you're both likable and lovable. That is gold. Now tell me what the heck it is that you've been dying to tell me but avoiding ever since you picked up your phone at the ungodly hour of five o'clock."

"I dreamt about Edward."

"You traveled back in time and visited your hunky Englishman," she corrected me.

"Yeah, whatever." Except she was right. If I hadn't believed I was time-traveling, if I had believed I was dreaming, then I wouldn't have gone all awkward-girl-meets-cute-boy. I wouldn't have felt like my seventeen-year-old self, complete with uncomfortable silences, bright blushes, and zero personality.

"How bad could it have been?" Slurping ensued, followed by a soft sigh. Someone was working on her caffeine fix. "You seemed into him, and your FG thinks he could be your one true love. It is literally her job to know stuff like that. Look at what a good job she did with Brad and me."

"Brad's the best," I agreed.

"Right, so what more do you need?"

It was like she didn't know me at all. "What more

do I need? For him not to think I'm an alien from another planet? For him never, ever to hear any of those stories, especially the Doug one, but also the costume ones."

"Pshaw. If he digs you, he'll dig your costumes... no matter how nerdy and unsexy they are." After a pause, she said, "But maybe we'll keep Doug between me and you."

"Exactly! It's bad enough that I have a real connection with a guy who lives in 1899 London, but then I had to go and ruin it by being me."

"By not being you, you mean. But I'm sure you didn't ruin it."

I huddled under my blanket and tried to think how it was possible I hadn't destroyed the tenuous connection building between Edward and me. Those relaxed conversations, quiet walks, and shared moments of humor were nothing when the conversation then became stilted, I could barely smile, and the silences turned weird and uncomfortable.

"Talk." The scrape of a chair meant that Hills was sitting down to enjoy her coffee. "Tell me how you've ruined everything."

"We could talk. My tongue didn't get all tangled. I didn't want to curl up and die every time we met. I think I ruined that." I tried to remember everything that had happened. "I showed up and just froze. It was a cool spring day, and I was sweating like crazy. He tried to talk to me, and I could barely utter a word."

"Oh, honey. It's not that bad. You had one bad date. That happens to everyone."

I snorted in disbelief. "It doesn't happen to *you*." Hills was so extroverted. So comfortable in her own skin. She was sexy and sweet and everyone liked her. Men *loved* her.

"Is that what you think? That I don't have days when I feel like everything I say is the wrong thing?"

That was exactly what I thought.

"Beth," she said, "you're not that special. Everyone feels awkward sometimes. Everyone stumbles over their words sometimes."

"Not as often as I do."

I could hear the smile in her voice when she replied, "That might be true, but only with men you find attractive."

She calmed my ruffled feathers in a way only Hillary could. My family didn't understand why I struggled in certain social situations, so while they were supportive, they didn't really get me.

Hillary might not suffer from any of my awkward issues, but she got it. She got me.

The Band-Aid she'd affixed to my battered psyche got me through the day, and I sent her a text that night thanking her for walking me away from the metaphorical cliff.

And then a few days passed with no time-traveling dreams. And then a few more.

That was weird. I thought it was weird. It probably was weird.

It didn't help that the last visit had been...less than ideal.

After a week and a half of Edward-less nights, I worked myself into a frenzy over the whole issue—to the point of making myself anxious about falling asleep.

And then—

Finally, I found myself in a quiet corner of a square garden. It looked like it might possibly be shared among a few houses. Edward was sitting on a bench sketching, completely absorbed by his task.

My heart raced. My tongue stuck to the roof of my mouth. My face heated. It was every bad crush on a cute, unattainable boy that I'd ever had, except ten times worse, because this wasn't a crush.

I liked Edward. I had feelings for him. And I couldn't help but feel like my terribly, painfully shy seventeen-year-old self. It was terrible.

Panic clutched at me, turning my stomach to a mess of cartwheeling butterflies. Butterflies *did* cartwheel. I knew, because it was happening inside me.

I couldn't catch my breath, and my chest got that tight feeling I hadn't felt in so very long.

No, no, no, no.

Just no.

I hadn't had a panic attack in what seemed like forever. I could not be having one now.

But I was.

I was having a panic attack in the middle of a garden, in London, in 1899.

Until I wasn't in 1899 London, and Edward was gone. I woke in my bed drenched with sweat.

Edward had been there, right in front of me, then he'd faded away, leaving me in the present with an aching heart and a sense that I'd lost something unique, something amazing, something I could never get back again.

12

BETH

This time I didn't call Hillary in a panic in the small hours of the morning.

I got up, ran, ate breakfast, and worked.

And then I went to bed knowing Edward wouldn't be waiting for me in my dreams.

Not to say I didn't hope. A kernel of stubborn hope remained, but I didn't really believe I'd see him again.

On day two, I got up, ran, ate breakfast, and worked.

Rinse and repeat for a week.

I was in a rut. A sad, tired rut, but not an anxious one. I'd have to hold more than a tiny, dying kernel of hope in my heart to be anxious. I'd have to believe

Edward and I had a real chance for anxiety to bubble up in all its panic-attack-inducing glory.

Edward and his quietly intelligent conversation and arm-porn-worthy arms seemed so very, very far away.

My phone pinged with a text from Hillary. She'd been sending me texts over the last few days, and while I'd tried to sound upbeat, I was refusing to answer some of her questions—which led to the phone calls that I was also refusing to answer.

If we chatted, she'd catch me in a lie, and I'd be lying if I told her I was all right. The alternative—the truth—wasn't really an option. I wasn't ready to talk about my might-have-been romance with Edward.

One kiss did not a romance make.

One kiss, a few conversations, some nice walks, that was all we'd had.

One amazing kiss, conversations filled with humor and understanding and a feeling of connection to another human being, and long walks filled with silences that were anything but awkward or tense.

Nope. Not ready to talk to Hillary about the amazing man I'd alienated by being a weirdo. Or was it the fickle hand of Fate that I'd pissed off? Or my FG? Whoever controlled my little jaunts back in time certainly wasn't happy with me right now.

Another text arrived, which I also ignored.

Then she called.

I didn't answer, and she texted me immediately: *Pick up or I'm coming over. And don't tell me you're not at home. I won't buy it.*

She must have drafted the dang text before she even called.

My phone rang again, and I answered this time.

Before I could muster a better-than-lackluster greeting, she asked, "Did I interrupt wild, uninhibited marathon sex?"

"What? No." Sometimes Hillary was living in her own reality. One where everyone had gobs of sex all day long.

"Did I wake you up from a steamy time-travel dream?"

"Nooo." And now she was just being weird with the sex-themed questions.

"All right, then there's only one reason you've been ducking my calls for the last few days. You're having Edward problems."

"An Edward problem implies there's an Edward and me. There is no Edward and me."

"Aw, honey. Maybe not yet, but Madeleine said there was a way for you and Edward to be together, so I'm sure there is. Don't let a setback or two get you down."

"A setback?" I sounded a little hysterical.

"Yeah, a hundred-plus years may *seem* like a big hurdle, but you have magic on your side."

"Ha! My 'setback' isn't related to the whole time-traveling, more-than-long-distance, magic-required part of my messed-up relationship with Edward." Someone might be feeling bitter right about now. And perhaps less than fond of anything related to magic or fairy godmothers.

"Um, no?"

Someone knocked on my front door.

I knew it was Hills, and I loved that when she was worried about me, she didn't take all my BS excuses; she just came over to my apartment to call me out on my fake-cheery texting and phone call avoidance.

When I opened the door, she wordlessly pulled me into a hug.

I cried.

She cried. Less than me, but she did, and Hills wasn't a crier.

After she handed me a dish towel, and I'd cleaned up my snotty self, she said, "Are you ready to tell me what's really happening now?"

I told her everything.

About the last time I'd seen Edward and how I'd slipped away before I was able to speak to him. She murmured words of sympathy.

About my panic attack being the cause of my

silence.

"Oh, honey. I'm so sorry. I didn't know you still got those."

"I don't." I bit my lip. "Not since high school."

Then I told her about not seeing Edward for days now.

She didn't have any words for that news, just hugged me again.

She busied herself making coffee and giving me a little more time to get myself together. When she sat down across from me at the kitchen table with two cups, she said, "Do you want me to be sympathetic—which I am; you know how much I want you to be happy—or do you want me to propose a next step?"

And once again, Hills was proving how well she knew me. I loved a good plan.

"Hit me. What have you got?"

"You need more practice."

I shook my head, because practice at what? Dating? We all knew that. And by we, I meant my entire high school graduating class, every boyfriend I'd had (all two of them), my family, and basically anyone who'd seen me interact with someone moderately attractive of the opposite sex.

I was a disaster. Not in life or work or as a friend, just as a member of the dating public.

She smiled. "I have just the thing. Let's hit that

coffee place around the corner."

"For coffee?" I glanced at the empty cup in front of me. I'd sucked it down hoping the liquid would warm the cold that had settled deep in my chest. "Because if I have any more caffeine, I might start vibrating."

Hillary snickered.

"From excess energy, you sex fiend. Stop looking at the world through your pervy filter for two seconds."

Elbows on the table, she rested her chin in her palms and flashed me one of her adorable grins. "I'm not pervy. I have a healthy relationship with my body and my need for sexual gratification on a very regular basis. So, coffee shop?"

I wrinkled my nose. I had a sneaking suspicion that I wasn't going to like whatever she had planned.

"You can get herbal tea, though I really want to see you vibrate. Heck, it's almost lunchtime. You can grab a snack with your hot beverage of choice."

The coffee place she was talking about was hip and always full of people around my age working on their laptops. People in their twenties, some of whom were guys. I suspected I knew where this was going, but I also knew whatever she concocted would distract me from my troubles, if only for a short while.

She sealed my fate when she leaned back in her

chair and said, "Look, I gave up awesome lunch sex with my smoking-hot boyfriend to come over here. You can't really say no."

"Fair point."

Which was how I ended up a half hour later sitting at my local coffee joint, sipping a tea, and commenting on the relative hotness of the men inside.

"How about that one?" Hillary asked, tipping her head toward another pretty boy on a laptop.

I wrinkled my nose. Sure, he was handsome, but he wasn't Edward handsome. "Edward's cuter."

Except Edward wasn't cuter, per se. Edward was incredibly attractive—and none of these guys were doing it for me.

Hillary set her coffee cup down with some deliberation, then leaned forward with a serious expression. "No one is going to be as attractive as Edward, because you're falling for Edward. You're a one-guy kinda girl, and that's a good thing simply because it's who you are."

Was it really a good thing? Given the circumstances—distance, time, our inability to be together even in dreams at this point—I was pretty sure it wasn't awesome.

When she didn't continue, I said, "But?"

"But we're here to practice, so put on your big-girl thong and let's pick a guy for you."

I winced. Practice sounded terrible. Really terrible, because she meant practice flirting...which required moving and talking and not acting like an introverted weirdo with no social skills.

I could just say no, except she was trying to help me, through distraction or desensitization or...gosh, I didn't even know, but however ridiculous she could sometimes be, she always had my back.

So with that in mind, I scanned the room and landed on the least intimidating guy I could find. "Right. That one."

Her eyebrows climbed. "I didn't know you were into tattoos. Or brawny men."

Tattoos and brawny men...what? I looked closer at the guy I'd indicated.

He was more casually dressed than some of the other guys and looked more relaxed, which was why I'd landed on him. But looking closer and with an objective eye, I could admit that he was actually pretty darn good looking in a manly way. Yeah, I kinda liked manly men. Edward had those incredible arms. I was baffled how a turn-of-the-century guy who walked in gardens and sketched had such nice arms.

But back to the tattooed, manly man in the casual clothes.

Contrary to Hillary's comment, he wasn't brawny. He did have a barbed-wire tat encircling a bicep that might fall into the arm-porn category...definitely fell into the arm-porn category.

I muttered a curse, which sparked a giggle from Hillary.

"You didn't even really see him, did you? You are so far gone. I'm gaga in love with Brad, and *I* looked."

I wasn't far gone. I wasn't gone at all. I'd met a nice man, who I found attractive and who I'd like to get to know better. Who made me smile and gave my heart flippy, warm-fuzzy feelings, and who was completely unattainable for so many reasons.

But the important part of all that was probably the flippy, warm-fuzzy-feelings part, regardless of his location—in time or space.

Ugh.

I was so far gone.

"What do you want me to do?" I asked with a weak smile.

Nothing big, as it turned out. Just hit on a very attractive man who was diligently working on his computer at the back of the coffee shop and clearly didn't want to be disturbed.

The pep talk that followed my reluctant agreement was awesome.

"Do you want to have sex with that man?"

I could feel my cheeks heat. "What? No!" I lowered my voice at the last moment so my denial came out more as a stage whisper than a holler.

She nodded with a satisfied look. "Of course you don't. You want to bang Mr. Victorian Hottie."

And now I was really blushing, because yes, I did. Inaccessible as he might currently be, I definitely wanted to bang Mr. Victorian Hottie.

"If hot tattoo guy hit on you, would you be really excited, jump up and down, and want to go to bed with him?"

I rolled my eyes, because clearly I wouldn't. We'd had the "one man at a time" conversation about two seconds earlier.

"Exactly," she replied with a big grin. "No pressure."

That didn't seem right to me. Just because I didn't want to sleep with an attractive man didn't mean he wasn't intimidating. It also didn't mean I wouldn't terribly embarrass myself if I tried to speak with him.

Before I could protest, Hillary grabbed my hand and squeezed it. "This is what you're going to do. You're going to the bathroom."

I nodded. I could definitely do that. Nerves, coffee, and now tea meant I was completely on board with that plan.

"On the way, you're going to pause."

That didn't seem terribly difficult.

"Next to him."

"Um..." That didn't seem like a good plan. "For what reason?"

She quirked an eyebrow.

"I mean, what's my cover story?"

Hills snorted and almost had coffee coming out of her nose. "This isn't a spy mission. You're going to the bathroom. You're pausing on the way, maybe to fiddle with your phone, and then when he looks up—and he will—you'll make eye contact, count to three, and then smile."

"Uh, then what?" Not that the plan didn't sound terrible already, but I knew the next steps would be worse. This was Hillary, after all. Did I have to grope his junk? Or ask for his number? Both equally terrifying propositions.

"Then you go to the bathroom and pee."

I blinked. "That's it?"

She patted my arm. "That's it."

So I did.

Mostly.

I counted to two very quickly, sort of smiled, blushed furiously, and then went to the bathroom.

Tattoo guy gave me a really nice smile when I came out of the bathroom—and then he went back to working on his laptop.

"Good girl," Hills said once I'd returned to the table. But she wouldn't let me sit down. "We're done here. We have a few other stops to make."

13

BETH

A few other stops had included another coffee shop, a café for a late lunch, a hopping pastry place that served great coffee and had lots of telecommuters squatting and mooching off the Wi-Fi, and finally a bar.

I smiled at a guy (without blushing!), flipped my hair over my shoulder while making intense eye contact (I definitely turned an unattractive shade of pink for that one), leaned in and touched a guy's arm, boob-brushed another guy's arm (after I had a glass of wine with lunch), and even sat down and chatted with a man over a drink at our last stop.

And—shockingly to me—I collected a few phone numbers along the way.

Hillary flagged down the shared ride driver after

double-checking the license plate and then opened the back door for me. "Hop in."

I'd only had two drinks, one with lunch and one at the bar, but she was insisting she had to escort me home before meeting Brad for dinner.

I settled in the far seat, and once she'd joined me and closed the door, she said, "I still can't believe you took a day off work to hand-hold me through a little flirting."

"Of course. Anything for my bestie, especially now that I have backup at work." The sparkle in her eye meant she was talking about Brad. "But what do you mean, a little flirting? Girl, you got three numbers!"

"Two."

Hillary whipped out a cocktail napkin from her purse with a gleeful grin. "Three. The bartender had the hots for you. Said to let you know he'd be way more fun than the boring guy in the striped tie."

Striped tie...which guy had a striped tie?

"The redhead, honey."

"Oh. Huh. He was with the guy who tried to buy me a drink. Is it normal that a guy I didn't even talk to wanted to buy me a drink?"

"The drink is the conversation starter, sweetie." She patted my arm. "I've tried to tell you, but you've never listened. You're gorgeous, you're friendly, and men absolutely notice you. You just don't notice them noticing you."

True statement on all counts. She had tried to tell me I was getting hit on, I'd never believed her, and now I had proof that Hillary wasn't completely full of it.

Not that I thought she was. I thought she'd been overly optimistic and also trying to bolster my self-confidence.

"How do you feel?"

I knew what the right answer was, so I supplied it. "More comfortable flirting with strange men."

"Uh-huh. And how do you really feel?" She arched a red eyebrow and leaned close enough that I could make out the almost-invisible dusting of freckles on her nose.

"Slightly more confident?"

She pursed her lips and waited.

Which led me to examine my feelings, rather than spitting out a best guess. Did I feel more confident? Actually...yes. But these men were strangers. "They weren't Edward."

"Yes. That was exactly the point." Her big blue eyes widened, producing a patently false expression of innocence. "Why? Were you thinking about giving any of them a call?"

I smacked her arm.

"Fine, you won't be calling them. But those poor

soon-to-be-disappointed men played a vital role. If you can talk to an attractive stranger, why can't you speak to a man who isn't a stranger at all? Someone who actually knows and likes you already?"

An excellent question, one I wouldn't have to answer, because we'd arrived at my apartment.

I put my hand on the seat belt buckle, waiting for the car to roll to a stop. "Gotta run."

"Beth." Hillary gave a look laden with meaning. Maybe a little judgment?

"I'm sorry. Thank you. For everything."

"No problem. That's what friends are for, and you know I had a blast. I've been wanting to do this for ages. I just never had strong enough leverage to get you to cooperate."

True. I wouldn't have left my comfort zone but for Edward. I wanted to give us a real chance, and not because some woman claiming to be my fairy godmother thought it was a good idea. Because I liked him. We had a connection, and I felt like we could have so much more.

And he was really attractive, the kind of attractive that made the butterflies in my stomach flutter and my lady parts pay attention. Very different from the cartwheeling butterflies that accompanied my panic attacks. (I had a complex relationship with butterflies.)

She lowered her voice and leaned closer, so our

nosy driver wouldn't hear her. "Edward is special. You'll sort out the long-distance issue, I'm sure of it, but you have to give the guy a chance."

"If I see him again," I mumbled.

Given my last time-traveling dream, I wasn't so sure I would.

14

EDWARD

Beth had slipped away without a word, and then a month passed.

Then another.

Two months.

Two lonely, empty months.

My life continued on, and as the days stretched by, one after another, it became apparent that I couldn't continue to live as I had since my sister's death.

I'd been drifting through my life, half-asleep and grieving. I'd isolated myself from the few friends I'd kept through the difficult time of Abigail's illness. I was alone in the world.

But then beautiful, sweet Beth had found her way to one of the few social events on my calendar, and she'd provided a glimpse into the life I might have. One with an attractive woman who understood me, who enjoyed my company, and whose companionship I craved.

She'd woken me to the possibilities of a fuller life...then disappeared.

At first, I was hopeful she would appear again. I half expected her around every corner, I looked for her in every park, but my hopes were frustrated time and again.

Then I was angry when she continued to stay away. She'd given me a gift then stolen it back. Selfishly, my thoughts were of *my* loss, *my* pain, *my* loneliness.

But the force that controlled Beth's appearance in my time, or her failure to appear, was one outside of her control. Magic or as-yet-undiscovered science, whatever the mechanism of her time travel, she could not will herself to 1899. And I began to question whether she suffered in her own time as I did in mine.

Except...she'd come and spoken not a word to me.

She'd arrived quietly inside the confines of my own garden—the first time she had appeared in or near my home—and without speaking one word, she'd faded away.

Had I offended her? Did she no longer wish to pursue our acquaintance? Or had words simply failed her?

Putting aside her lack of speech, why the painfully short duration of her visit? Always before when she'd visited, she'd been in my time for many minutes, even hours. This time, her appearance had lasted no more than a minute, perhaps less. I didn't believe she'd even been aware I spotted her before she again disappeared.

Beth had no control over her appearances in my time, of this I was almost certain. But accepting this truth allowed my anger to dissipate, and with its loss I became achingly aware of the hole in my life, in my heart. While the emptiness I felt had begun with my parents' deaths, then grown with Great-Aunt Celia's and finally Abigail's, for a time, Beth had filled it up with her light.

I missed her.

But I could not continue to live a half existence. I owed my aunt, my sister, every person who had ever loved me, more than that. I owed myself more.

So I ventured once again into society. I considered the single women of my acquaintance. I considered their suitability as partners, and while I could not bring myself to land upon any viable candidates, at least I was looking.

Did they fail to capture my attention? Or did I fail in opening my heart to the possibility of them? I was unsure.

After I had no success in finding a partner, a second campaign was born. Friendship was also an important lack in my current life. I attended events, I renewed old acquaintanceships, I tried—as best I could—to allow myself to truly know some of the people in my circle, men and women.

Several cordial conversations followed, a handful of turns around the ballroom that weren't entirely uncomfortable, and a few evenings of cards that, while not enjoyable, were certainly bearable.

All interactions paled in comparison to my meetings with Beth.

While many of the ladies in my circle were accomplished and beautiful, none elicited the same physical attraction I felt for Beth. And I failed to hold a conversation, with man or woman, that ventured beyond the state of the weather or expectations regarding my attendance at future social functions.

Pleasant. That best described my interactions with members inside my own social circle.

I desired more than pleasant. I wanted—needed—to fill the emptiness that lived within my heart. Beth made me feel less alone, and I wanted that. Quite badly, in fact.

And I was beginning to believe, absent Beth's return, that I would fail in my search.

15

BETH

A gentle swaying motion rocked me, and through a sleepy haze I thanked the stars and my mom—whose iron stomach I'd inherited—for my immunity to motion sickness.

Combine my swaying, creaking environment with the rhythmic sound of hooves on cobblestones, and on some level of consciousness I registered I was riding in a carriage.

It was surprisingly pleasant right up until the vehicle jarred my bones so hard that I thought I'd lose a tooth.

A startled sound escaped my mouth at about the same time I realized I was sitting in a small, confined space across from the man I'd been falling topsy-turvy in crush with. Maybe more than in crush, but I couldn't really consider that possibility with him within arm's reach in an enclosed carriage. I preferred not to lose the power of speech.

Except...

I thought I'd never see him again, and he was *right here*.

I let loose a breath I was pretty sure I'd been holding for thirteen days.

"Beth." Edward's wary gaze met mine. "Good afternoon."

Right. My last two visits had been less than stellar. Although at least he didn't see me the last time. Wouldn't that have been mortifying? Having an actual panic attack witnessed by my possible one true love.

Uh-huh, I was totally on board with Madeleine's One True Love pitch. Romantic me was, anyway. Practical me *wanted* to believe, but she was waiting for more evidence.

"Have circumstances changed such that you're no longer able to converse while in my time? I worried, after your last visit, that this might be true."

Oops. Yeah, he'd definitely seen me. Two visits gone bad, one with me stuttering and one with me panic-attacking in the corner.

Humiliating? Yes.

Speech-inhibiting and panic-inducing? Umm...

Another breath escaped and the tension in my shoulders eased, because no. I was not currently having a panic attack. And if I wasn't losing my marbles, then I could likely speak. And the poor man was starting to look really stressed out by my continued silence.

"Beth?"

I met his gaze and made my lips move. "I'm fine." And with those words safely out in the open, I realized I really was. "I don't always know the right thing to say, and so I…"

"Don't speak?" He reached for my hand and kissed it.

The man kissed my hand. If I were standing, I might have taken a cue from the too-tight corset-wearing women of the Victorian age and swooned, because Edward Stanbury kissing my hand was downright swoon-worthy.

Slightly breathless for reasons other than anxiety, I said, "It's silly, I know."

"No." He squeezed my fingers. He could do that because he hadn't let go of my hand yet. Did I mention sworn-worthy? That was my man.

Ohmigod. And now I was talking like he was mine, and I was going to keep him. Like I could keep him. As if he didn't live in 1899—another freaking time, for crying out loud.

I was back to losing my marbles again, just walking down the delusional path instead of the anxiety-laden one.

In my defense, the carriage was small, Edward was holding my hand, and he smelled divine.

Also, I'd been practicing the whole flirting thing, which was supposed to make me braver. I should definitely be brave when the guy I was gaga over was giving me green-light eyes. And by green-light I mean heavy with desire, but also filled with all sorts of other yummy emotions that I couldn't quite parse but all seemingly of the good variety.

Enough mooning. Time to channel Hillary and put my big-girl thong on, metaphorically. Literally, I was clothed in some version of a travel suit, because magic was weird and liked to clothe me in period-appropriate garb.

I was doing this.

I was.

Right now.

And I did.

I yanked Edward's hand hard. I might not be working out at the gym much or have bulging biceps like a certain hunky Victorian gent, but my slight frame masked some freakish strength.

One stout pull and I had a lap full of delicious-smelling man.

And this was the part I wouldn't forget, whether we never saw each other again and I was clinging to this as my last memory of Edward (said practical me), or if we fell in love and got married and had babies and adopted dogs and moved to the perfect house with the perfect yard (romantic me).

Either way, this was one for the memory banks.

Edward used those athletic arms and some truly exceptional balance and core strength to gracefully flip our positions so that he was on the carriage seat and I was sitting in his lap. And, with no hesitation at all, the man kissed me.

This was no chaste pressing of lips together.

This was full-on, R-rated kissing. Hillary would be so proud.

But I wasn't thinking about strength, grace, Hillary, or anything else, because Edward's woodsy scent surrounded me. The masculine strength of his arms encircled me. And his mouth, his lips, consumed me.

The Victorian gentleman was gone, and this Edward—a breathy sigh escaped my lips—was making me melt.

As our tongues tangled together, he pressed me closer to his body—his very hard, very male body.

I wiggled closer, feeling anything but shy or embarrassed. Speechless, yes, but only because—yum. Edward was delicious in every way.

And then I woke up.

16

BETH

"Noooo!"

What kind of magic left me hot and bothered and alone in my bed on an otherwise innocuous Tuesday morning?

The crappy, mean-spirited kind, that was what kind.

And when did I start to channel twelve-year-old girls who throw temper tantrums?

I bounced out of bed, ready to punch some people. But since that wasn't feasible and I was generally a nonviolent kind of person—actually, really nonconfrontational—I called Hillary instead.

"Do you have any idea what time it is?" Hillary's sleep-befuddled voice held a hint of crankiness. "Two mornings in a row. I might start not answering."

"Seriously? You know, I actually checked this time, and it's after eight. You should be up." Weirdly, I'd slept through my alarm.

Or maybe not weird, since I was going at it with a certain Victorian hottie?

She grumbled about recovering from the previous night's lack of sleep, which was completely hokey. On the Hillary scale of tiring, yesterday had been a piece of cake. No juggling of four businesses, since her honey had managed everything while she took a day off, and she'd probably gotten a good six hours of sleep, which well exceeded her pre-Brad days.

"You're getting soft. Since you started dating Brad, it's like you're almost not a workaholic."

She made a satisfied noise that sounded way too much like a purr.

"Hills, get your mind out of the gutter. We're focusing on *my* sex life now. Catch up."

"What?" she shrieked. "I'm awake. I'm paying attention. Tell me everything. Ohmigod, you had a sex dream. I mean, you had sex, but not in a dream because it was real. Yay!"

It was like someone had recorded her voice and was playing it back at time-and-a-half speed.

I snorted. Not that it was any great surprise that Hillary was on Team Get Beth Laid, but it was still pretty funny how excited she was. "Um, not quite."

"But you time-traveled."

"I did. And thank you so much for all your help, because I didn't have a panic attack. I even managed to speak."

"Ha! Girl, sounds like you did more than speak. Did you at least get some quality Os?"

Os plural? Wait, what? Was that a thing? I knew better than to ask, because then our conversation would be completely derailed, and we'd be talking about my past, my sadly multiple-O-lacking past. I wanted to talk about my future, thank you very much.

"We kissed, and it was amazing. But get this...I made the first move." Then I waited for the explosion.

"Oh. My. God. My little girl is all grown up!" Her statement was followed by a squeal of excitement.

"I thought you'd be excited." I didn't want to rain on her parade, but... "Small problem. I woke up midkiss."

"Oh." Her proclamation was followed by silence.

Best to let her absorb the news. She might tease me about my process when it came to handling change, but she had her own process related to disappointment.

"Okay, I think I'm good."

I gave her another few seconds. Was that a sniffle I heard? I rolled my eyes, because, first of all, she couldn't see me, and second, how could I not?

She sighed. "I mean, you know I'm sad for you, but I think the shock is wearing off."

"Uh-huh. So we can talk strategy?"

"Yes, absolutely. I'm so excited that you're finally coming out of your shell. But yes, let's plan. Planning is your jam, and I can do that."

Hillary got me. I loved that she got me. "Okay, long story short, I'm here and he's there. How do we fix that, since your FG won't actually tell us how to make that happen?"

"There has to be a way, or she wouldn't have introduced the two of you and let you fall in love."

"Um, love?" Feelings, yes. But love? I couldn't go there. Not yet. Not while Edward was in 1899 and I was here. Not when every chance we had to talk, to touch, to kiss, was dependent on some fickle magic woo-woo fairy dust that I didn't understand or even fully believe in.

"Yes, love, Beth. Two hearts beating as one. Your very special person who gets you and makes you want to tear his clothes off. What else are we talking about?"

"I'm not in love. Even your FG said that Edward was a *possibility* for my one true love."

"Not just *a* possibility, the *best* possibility. And you have feelings for him, don't you?"

I swallowed the lump of fear in my throat. "Yes, but how can I fall in love with a man whose existence I'm not entirely certain of? Whose continued presence in my life is a complete unknown? Who may not be there tomorrow, because he's certainly not here today?"

"Honey, you need to think about what you want. You seem to be straddling the fence right now. Do you want Edward enough to believe in him?"

That was unfair. So, so unfair. How could I be all in when there was no certainty that Edward was even *real*?

I *thought* he was, but I didn't *know* it.

17

EDWARD

The bed I occupied was not my own.

Narrow, comfortable but firm, and with an unfamiliar texture. All of these details registered within my mind before I woke fully.

I opened my eyes to find myself in a room I didn't recognize, resting upon a settee. It was no great surprise I'd thought myself in bed. The cushions of the settee were more comfortable than any in my own home.

A feeling of disorientation muddled my thoughts momentarily. I had no recollection of waking, rising from bed, dressing, or leaving my home.

And the clothing I wore... It wasn't mine. It didn't belong to me, but more than that, I'd never seen its like before. I ran my hand down the dark blue fabric of my pants. It looked rough but was surprisingly comfortable. My shirt was made of a dark, buttery-soft fabric and only partially covered my upper arms. My shoes were dark and so lightweight and flexible that I felt almost as if I wore no shoes at all. I balanced on my toes and rocked back on my heels. Quite comfortable. But I felt only half-dressed.

Dressing for comfort, a topic I'd discussed with Beth on more than one occasion. And as that idea permeated my conscious thought, I ceased examining my clothing and turned all of my attention to the room I occupied.

It appeared to be an informal parlor. Though some of the contents of the room were familiar, even those items were touched by strangeness. And there were several pieces whose function eluded me.

The furniture was identifiable—the settee, a side table, two chairs—but the styles were unfamiliar. Framed pictures were sprinkled throughout the room, but each photo was in startling color. I peered more closely at the one nearest to me and touched my finger to the flawless glass.

As I considered a large, flat rectangle occupying a place of honor on its own piece of furniture (perhaps an empty frame waiting for a picture?), a tremendous rumble echoed through the room. The sound had come from outside, so I moved to yet another wonder, a huge window with glass so fine that it appeared to be air.

Distracted by the quality of the huge windows, I failed to pinpoint the origin of the noise. I did discover I was on the second floor of a house that was somewhat larger than the other houses on the street. All of the other homes had a sameness, as if designed by the same architect. Each had a small plot of grassy lawn and a tiny garden. This house, however, had an expanse of paved road with lines painted on it instead of the grass the other homes had cultivated.

Based on the position of the sun, it was near midday, a time when the daily activities of a household should be at their peak, and yet this street held none of that hectic energy. No nannies pushed prams; no maids hurried to complete errands.

As I contemplated what that meant, what the fine glass and strange furniture meant, a box on wheels sped down the street. I scrambled away from the window. Fearful of being seen by the people inside? Perhaps.

I took a breath and renamed the object as my heart thudded in my chest. It was no box, but a motorcar. Bigger, faster, sleeker than any I'd seen before, but still a motorcar. During our talks, Beth had explained many advances in science, including changes in transportation. Experiencing it firsthand, however, was...unsettling.

It was past time I found some answers concerning my whereabouts. Whose home was I occupying? And how distressed would they be to find an uninvited visitor should they return home?

The photos. Surely that hadn't changed over time. The photos in this home had to give some indication as to the occupant.

The one I'd already inspected had been of a dog, not that I'd taken great notice, as focused as I'd been upon the quality of the picture. I scanned the room looking for another that might be more revealing... and victory.

I picked up my prize, a moment in time captured, full of color and life. The photo showed a young woman with a tidy, almost severe appearance standing close to an older man in an oddly tailored suit and an older woman displaying a good expanse of bare leg.

But these were merely passing thoughts. The young woman held my attention. Elizabeth. A younger, less feminine version of the woman I'd come to know. She was covered from shoulder to toe in a long, black, bulky garment that resembled the robes of a university student.

I'd traveled to the future and landed inside Elizabeth's home.

How?

What had I done differently to be allowed this opportunity?

Did I even care, so long as I saw Beth?

Yes. Yes, I did care. Because I suspected this trip would end at some point. If my trip was like Beth's, it would come to a close with no warning. And I wanted to come back. I wanted to see Beth as often and for as long as possible.

I replaced the photograph gently on the table.

Where was she? I'd landed in her home, but there was no sign of her. I thought she worked here, and the large table in her kitchen was littered with what appeared to be papers and books associated with her work, and yet there was no sign of her.

Every time Beth had visited my time, she'd appeared before me. No, that wasn't right. Every time except the first.

The first time, I'd found her in the garden and couldn't be sure how long she'd been outside. It could have been some time, given her account of the night. She'd been disoriented by the environment, her clothes, being unexpectedly in a strange place. In fact, her experience had been markedly similar to the one I was having now.

She'd been outside only feet away from me when she arrived in my time, and I hadn't yet called out for her or searched the immediate area.

"Beth?" I waited a few seconds then called her name again, louder, but there was no response.

The situation called for exploration, because clearly Beth wasn't here.

After a quick—and, I hoped, not intrusive—search of her home, I headed for the front door. The bathroom was a thing of beauty with its oversized mirror and sparkling tiles. And the kitchen... Beth had described cold storage for food, but I'd envisioned something more like a cupboard, something similar to the ice houses of my day but much smaller. I most certainly hadn't envisioned the reality, a gleaming metal monstrosity of an object.

After I completed my search indoors, it was clear Beth's home was a flat within a much larger house. As I expected, the front door led into an interior hallway of the larger home in which the flat was situated. There was only one other flat on this floor, and a set of stairs.

Before I could decide whether to descend the stairs and continue my search or wait for Beth inside, a young woman popped her head out of the door of the other flat.

She lifted her hand, waved excitedly, and called out a greeting. I reciprocated the gesture in a more subdued manner before retreating back inside Beth's flat.

I had no understanding of this society. Would my

exiting Beth's flat create difficulties for Beth? In light of the neighbor's overt interest, the safest course of action seemed to be to remain out of sight.

A crack pierced the air, followed by the rumble of an engine. This time when I looked out the window, I saw the similarities to the modern version of the motorcars from my time.

I'd ridden in one once. They were hardly common in 1899 England. Motorcars in my day were open-air carriages with engines. This car was so much sleeker, so much faster.

Common sense dictated that science would move forward, and Beth had on several occasions provided specific details of modern advances. But to be confronted with the reality was something altogether different.

Thank goodness I lived in an era of industrial accomplishment and scientific advancement. Had I been born a hundred years earlier, I could imagine the differences between Beth's time and my own would be that much more difficult to comprehend.

Another motorcar whizzed by, and then another, which raised the question: had the scientists of today resolved the ill effects traveling at such high speeds had upon the body?

The thought of being trapped in a fast-moving metal box while my organs bounced around inside my body made my skin prickle with unease. Not that

I would have to ride in one. I was, after all, only a visitor to this time.

But that thought made me even more uncomfortable. I had no family left, no ties to the world in which I lived. And one of us would have to live in the other's time.

Assuming there was a choice involved, it would be an easy one for me to make. I would gladly leave behind my life for a new one with Beth, even if that meant wearing workman's trousers and what looked like little more than an undershirt, or riding in speeding motorcars, or living in a flat that was roughly one-tenth the size of my current home.

Working—as I knew I would have to in this day and age—would be challenging. As a man of independent means, I wasn't trained in a profession. But I would find a way to persevere and succeed, because Beth would be the reward.

Whether she felt the same...that was a question I couldn't, wouldn't, ask her.

18

BETH

"Thanks for having me over." I tugged Walter into a hug before he ushered me into the kitchen.

"I'm glad to have you. It's been too long."

"Gramps," Hillary called from the depths of the house. "Do you mind getting Beth a drink?"

Walter raised his eyebrows at that. "Rough morning?"

I couldn't blame him for asking. It was only two o'clock, much too early for me to be off work for starters, and definitely a bit early for a drink.

"Definitely a rough morning."

"Whiskey, beer, wine or mixed-drink rough?"

Which made me laugh, because I'm not sure what a whiskey-rough day looked like. I didn't drink straight whiskey.

"What have you got for cocktail fixings?"

Hillary appeared in the kitchen just in time to announce, "We have all the cocktail fixings. You know we've been hosting the family regularly for dinners, right? That is a cocktail-drinking kind of event."

"Be nice." Walter's admonishment carried little weight considering he delivered it with twitching lips. The man was trying his best not to smile.

Hillary shrugged. "We love them, but they're a pain in the tush. Admit it, Gramps. And she'll have a vodka gimlet."

Walter looked at me for confirmation.

"Sure." I'd had one the day Hillary had been "flirtation training" me, and it had been pretty good.

As Walter mixed the drink, Hillary pulled me to the kitchen table. "We can kick Gramps out if you don't want to talk about the good stuff in front of him."

The good stuff? I wouldn't consider my current romantic dilemma "good stuff."

"I don't know. If he doesn't mind hearing all the sordid details, maybe he can give me some advice." I gave Hillary a meaningful glance. "Some sane advice."

Hills snorted. "From the guy who lived with an imaginary friend for years. Uh-huh. My feelings might be hurt if I didn't know how wise Gramps is."

Walter delivered my gimlet, a lemonade for Hillary, then sat down in front of the coffee he must have abandoned when I first arrived. "Glad to hear I'm wise, but my friend wasn't imaginary, as you well know." He gave Hillary a pointed look. "What kind of advice am I doling out?"

"Beth some guidance in her romantic life."

Gramps's eyebrows raised. "From a retired guy who hasn't been on a date in over fifty years?"

"Advice about love, Gramps, not dating."

And the distinction was pretty important, because if anyone knew about love, Walter Barrett did. He'd married the love of his life, and for over fifty years they'd had an amazing marriage. Not without challenges, of course, but he and his wife had the kind of marriage that I wished for in the deepest part of my heart: filled with love, understanding, compromise, support, and so much affection.

The loss of his wife Ingrid had been the trigger for his imaginary friend's creation...or so we'd all thought until recently.

I loved Walter, trusted him, and yet... Magic fairy dust, wicked witches, and curses?

"Ah. I didn't know you'd met someone." He turned his kind eyes and the weight of *all* of his attention to me.

Which naturally made me squirm. In part

because I'd been sitting across from him doubting the narrative of his recent life changes.

Also, because his question hit on the crux of my problem. Had I met someone, or had I imagined someone? Time travel only occurred in fiction. Fairy godmothers were a bunch of boloney. Handsome, kind men with muscular arms, a delicious woodsy scent, and an incredible accent who happened to be smitten with me only existed in my dreams.

And I was a huge coward, because believing in my very own happily ever after seemed too risky. It simply couldn't be true.

When my silence continued a beat too long, Walter said, "Or you haven't met someone?"

"Um, I'm not exactly sure."

"You're not sure of your feelings?" He sipped his coffee, but never took his eyes off me. When I was a kid and would tag along with Hillary to play in Walter's huge yard, he always seemed to get me.

While I considered the best way to convey my concerns without hurting his feelings, Hillary just jumped right in. "Beth's met a hot guy that lives in Victorian England. Madeleine set her up."

"Oh, well that's surprising." But he didn't look exactly shocked. He took a (very calm) sip of his coffee and looked at me.

"They're just dreams." My chest tightened as I said the words.

"Oh?"

That's all Walter said, just "oh," but that's all it took for my eyes to get watery.

I would *not* cry. "I kept waking up in 1899 England, and Edward was always there."

"Edward?"

With that single prompt, Walter had me spilling all the beans. What Edward looked like, how kind he was, that he was all alone in the world after losing first his parents then his great-aunt and finally his sister, that we clicked on a level I'd never before experienced.

A blush stained my cheeks as I fessed up to that last part, and I gave Hillary the hairy eyeball. "And I'm not just talking about sexual attraction."

"Not just..." Hillary said with a grin.

Dang it, she got me there. It took a second for me to be able to meet Walter's eyes—he was Hillary's grandfather, for goodness sakes—but when he cleared his throat, I lifted my gaze.

With only a tiny spark of amusement in his eyes, he said, "It sounds like Edward is a fine man."

"*Was*, maybe? If he's even real, which he can't be because... Magic? Fairies?"

Walter said, "Fairy godmother" at the same time that Hillary said, "FG."

Which made me roll my eyes, because what had I been expecting? They'd both boarded the same crazy train and were happily riding it into the sunset.

"Why can't it be true?" Walter asked. "Because magic is an impossibility, or because you don't believe in the possibility of your own happily ever after?"

My heart thudded in my chest. "That's not fair, Walter."

I wanted love. I wanted to find my own Brad or Ingrid—my other half—but it wasn't that easy. Some random fairy didn't just wave her magic wand and then an amazingly perfect man fell in love with me. Please.

Very quietly, he said, "I agree one hundred percent."

Wait, what?

I rewound and replayed our conversation. "Hold on. Just because I think fairy godmothers are hokey doesn't mean that I don't think I deserve my own happy ending."

"Deserve?" Hillary blinked at me then looked at Walter, and for the first time since I'd told her about Edward she looked really upset. Sad, even. "It's not a question of deserving or not deserving. Love is for everyone, Beth. But I think Gramps hit the nail on the head. Take magic completely out of the equation, and what would you do?"

"I don't understand." Without magic, there's no

Edward in my life. He lived in England, *in another time*.

"You meet Edward in a bar or maybe he's a client. You guys hit it off, and then...what happens? Do you grab that opportunity with both hands, or do you just let him float away, another lost chance?" She peered at me with a hard look in her eyes.

"That's not fair. I'd never meet a guy like Edward in a bar or at work and hit it off." And we both knew why. Heck, even Walter knew why. I was too shy for the first scenario, and my no-dating-clients rule prohibited the second.

Although I *had* recently gotten a few phone numbers at a bar, and I *could* bend my self-imposed no-dating-clients rule.

Hills tapped a fingernail on the kitchen table, then stopped abruptly and downed the rest of her lemonade. "I need a whiskey. You're stressing me out."

I was stressing *her* out?

When she came back with a whiskey and soda—mostly soda, so I wasn't stressing her out that much—she said, "So? You meet Edward in real life, and...?"

"And you're both right. I've always assumed that would never happen, because it never has." I wrinkled my nose as my cheeks flushed. "Walter, you may not be aware, but I met my previous boyfriends under sort of special circumstances."

He waited for me to explain, but Hills wasn't so patient. "She's dated two guys. One was her high school lab partner, and the other was the RA her sophomore year."

"Hey," I protested. "We didn't date until my junior year when he wasn't my RA anymore."

"Moot," Hills replied.

Walter nodded. "Lots of time to get to know them with little pressure. It's just too bad that neither of them was the One."

Nail-head, Walter was on the ball.

"True statement, Walter. And to answer your question, Hills, I like to think if I'd met Edward here, in my real life, and we had the same connection I feel with dream Edward, that, yes, I'd grab ahold with both hands."

19

BETH

I ended up staying for an early dinner with Walter and Hillary after our little "chat."

Walter loved feeding visitors. He claimed he liked the practice; Hillary said he liked to show off his newly acquired cooking skills (Brad's influence). I had to shake my head—because Brad—but I appreciated him making sure I was safe to drive and well-fed.

My day had taken an unusual path. I started with an unproductive morning, then I followed that up with the disturbing realization that the stress in my life had risen to such levels that it was affecting my work. Then I'd examined the stressors in my life—essentially dreams and the emotions they'd evoked—and then I'd had a proper freak-out.

There existed within me two completely incompatible beliefs: Edward and the feelings I had for him were real, and magic didn't—couldn't—exist.

Cue Hillary and her recent ability to bend and twist her schedule at will—thank you, Brad, and the employees he'd helped Hillary hire—and I'd landed on her doorstep.

Then Walter had pointed out the obvious, that I was a big ol' loser who didn't even believe in myself.

The whole way home, I'd given myself a pep talk. I was awesome. I was a confident woman. I was capable of dating, and even more, I was capable of love. I was worthy of love. Blah blah blah.

The interior of my car was like a self-help meeting, speaker and attendee, all in one. Yep, I'd given myself that pep talk one hundred percent out loud.

When I opened my front door, I was still muttering happy, empowering words. Something along the lines of, "My heart is open and ready for love."

That's when I heard someone say my name.

Someone who entered my living room a split second later.

Tall, clean-shaven, wearing jeans and a fitted T-shirt, my dream man was less than ten feet away and getting closer.

Except, no, he wasn't—because Edward wasn't real. Edward lived in my dreams. Edward did not live in Austin, Texas. In the present. In my living room.

Two worlds collided.

Two conflicting beliefs clashed.

Which naturally made the floor tilt, the walls wobble, and my breath freeze in my lungs.

I was hallucinating. That was the only explanation.

Walter had spiked my drink with something besides booze. Hillary had hypnotized me and planted a suggestion in my brain. The aliens had landed, and they looked like Edward. Yeah, not going to claim this as my proudest moment, because all of those thoughts actually flitted, ever so briefly, through my head.

Panicked me had a great sense of humor.

"Beth?" Hallucination/hypnotic suggestion/alien Edward was still here, except now he was standing directly in front of me and looking more than a little worried, maybe even freaked out.

I inhaled, intending to speak, though I hadn't gotten so far as the actual words I would utter, and that's when I achieved clarity. Because hallucination/hypnotic suggestion/alien Edward smelled like Edward. Plain old (yet deliciously yummy) Edward.

Actually, clarity might be an exaggeration. I did, however, feel grounded enough to reach out and test whether the man in front of me was as solid as he seemed or a multisensory hallucination.

And when I say touch, what I really mean is

squeeze. I might have groped a bicep, but in my defense, I'd never seen Edward in anything less than a full Victorian suit of clothes, and those arms in that T-shirt... Well, suffice it to say, I couldn't *not* grope.

And the man in front of me was definitely real. Warm to the touch, built like an athlete, and looking less concerned by the minute.

After the third squeeze, he grinned. "I'm real."

Whew. At least he understood my need for tactile confirmation and didn't think I was a complete perv. Or maybe he did and was too much of a gentleman to comment.

When I removed my hand—there was some serious willpower at play—he looked down at his shirt and then examined my dress. "I might be able to guess how disorienting it was for you to arrive in my world dressed as a Victorian woman." With a quick touch of the shirt's collar and then the denim pants, he said, "Can I assume I'm appropriately attired for your world?"

Which made me want to smile, because he was scandalously clothed by Victorian standards. "Definitely. It's warm outside. Most men wear short sleeves this time of year in Austin. I can find you something else to wear, if you're uncomfortable."

He shook his head. "But thank you for the offer."

I couldn't help looking around my apartment

and wondering how he saw it. It had to be so much smaller and plainer than his own home. It had been clear that Edward was an affluent man in his time. "How long have you been here?"

"An hour, perhaps two." He pressed his lips together. "A lady across the hall saw me when I opened the front door. Will that be a problem for you?"

"No, no problem." But then I blushed, because I didn't want him to think I had men crashing at my apartment regularly, not that there was anything wrong with that, but I didn't like the idea that he...oh my gosh. I was officially losing it. With a smile, I said, "I don't have a lot of company, so she may have been surprised, but that's all."

"Good." He nodded.

We were about two seconds from heading into the land of awkward, a place I was very familiar with and one I didn't want to visit.

And naturally, that's the moment my brain decided to remind me that Edward. Was. Here.

As in, he wasn't a dream.

Real guy, in my living room, having a conversation with me, dressed like any other guy walking down the street in Austin.

What was happening right now? Because I was definitely awake.

And then the universe decided it wanted to get

its giggles in for the day, because that's when I remembered swearing to my best friend that I would absolutely grab ahold of Edward if I were to meet him in my real life and we had the same connection.

We were in real life. Definitely in the present, certainly in my own apartment, and I was so completely awake right now.

Hills asked if I would grab ahold...metaphorically.

Except why not literally? That sounded good to me. Great, in fact.

So I did.

20

EDWARD

She kissed me.

Not a peck on the cheek or a tentative brushing of lips. She grabbed the material of my shirt with both hands, tugged me closer, and when I didn't lower my head fast enough, she stretched up on her toes and tugged my head down.

When our lips met, all my hesitation vanished. No, not hesitation, because I would gladly kiss Beth whenever the opportunity arose. My surprise faded, and I participated—right up until she opened her mouth and gently bit my lip.

Then there was no question of hesitation, surprise, or participation. I pulled her tight against my body, palmed the back of her head, and devoured her lips.

Our tongues tangled, our hands wandered, and

we only paused when we were both gasping for breath.

Our foreheads touched, and with a hitch in her breath, she whispered, "What just happened?"

My lips stretched into a huge grin. The wonder in her voice allayed any fears I might have had that she regretted our actions. "I believe you just ravished me."

She snorted as she laughed. It was an endearing sound, but it must have embarrassed her because she tucked her face against my neck.

It seemed an excellent opportunity to hold her close. I wrapped my arms around her and rubbed her back in what I hoped were soothing circles. *I* wasn't soothed. The prolonged contact with her feminine curves and the gentle puff of her breath on my neck were making my trousers increasingly uncomfortable, but I wouldn't forgo our contact to allay such slight discomfort.

After a few minutes passed, she eventually spoke, her lips moving against my neck. "I told my best friend that if you lived here in my world that I wouldn't hesitate to grab you with both hands." Her laughter tickled my skin. "We were speaking in a more metaphorical sense, but she'll be thrilled."

I didn't have a response. Her words, *if you lived here*, echoed through my head, because I didn't live in this world. I was a visitor, dependent upon unknown means for transportation and unsure even of the length of my trip.

When my silence continued, Beth stepped away from the circle of my arms. "What's wrong?"

I rubbed my thumb along her jaw. "I thought it difficult to wait for your appearance, never knowing when you would arrive, but it's equally difficult to be here with you, not knowing when it will suddenly end."

She cupped my hand and held it against her face then let go. "That's why we need a plan. This calls for a drink."

She led me into her small, shiny kitchen, and filled a colorful kettle which she then plugged into the wall.

"Everything is electric?" It was fascinating to see electricity used in so many ways. My own home had electric lighting but nothing more.

"Or gas, yes." As she rummaged in her cupboard, she asked, "Is tea all right?"

"Yes, thank you."

She must have heard the smile in my voice, because she paused in her search and looked over her shoulder. "What?"

I shook my head. "Tea. With all of the advancements—electricity, your cooling cupboard, motor-wagons—tea remains. It's comforting."

She grinned. "Well, it's not quite as common

here as it is in England or even in the north of the United States, but everyone definitely still drinks tea." Her head disappeared once again into the cupboard. "I would have offered you a glass of wine or a cocktail, but I wasn't sure if you drink."

"I do, but tea is perfect."

"Aha. Here it is. I've got English breakfast and Earl Grey." She proudly flourished two small boxes, but then wrinkled her nose. "I doubt that it's very good tea, so you're forewarned."

The kettle made a clicking noise, and she set about preparing English breakfast.

As predicted, it wasn't very good, but I appreciated her efforts. Also, the simple task had allowed her time to recover from our moment of intimacy. Beth might have initiated the kiss, but that didn't mean she'd be any more comfortable in its aftermath.

She was adorably, endearingly shy, while also being forthright and confident. The juxtaposition might seem unlikely, but it was simply how she was —and she was perfect.

We sat at the kitchen table and quietly drank our tea for a few minutes. I hadn't had tea in the kitchen since I was a small child, and I'd never drunk from such large, utilitarian mugs. It was homey; I liked it very much.

She bit her lip and examined me while she

fiddled with her mug. "Are you okay? I mean, you mentioned the fridge—the cooling cupboard—and motorwagons and the electricity, but it's more than that. My apartment has to feel weird to you. Your life is my history, but my life hasn't happened for you yet. I'm sure that's...well, that it's overwhelming."

I finished my tea and set the mug aside. "More than a hundred years has passed, and a great number of advancements have been made. But some customs," I glanced at our tea mugs, "however unpopular, remain unchanged."

"I'd think more is different than is the same, especially since you're no longer in England."

"I'm not so certain that's true." I allowed myself a moment to pinpoint the facts supporting my conclusion. "Your nosy neighbor."

"Rebecca." Beth rolled her eyes. "She was probably in shock that someone other than Hillary or my family was visiting."

"But nosy neighbors exist in my world, as well." I knocked a knuckle on her table. "You have a kitchen to cook in, a dining table at which you eat, a bathroom with more gleaming fixtures, but yet still a place where you bathe."

She tipped her head, so I continued. "Workers still rise in the morning and travel to their workplace?"

"Yes, except some work from home."

"Also a possibility in my time, though from what you've explained to me of your own work, I suspect the type of work performed varies."

"Okay, okay. You've convinced me. The present is exactly like the past, but shinier." An oversimplification of my point, but a humorous one. All levity vanished as she sat back in her chair, a determined look on her gorgeous face. "Does that mean you're ready to talk about a plan?"

I needed clarity. *I* was committed to a future with the two of us, but was *she*? Of the two of us, she had always been the one less certain of the reality of our situation. I had believed almost from the beginning, in her, in a possible future between us, whereas she had to be reminded of our "bargain": I behaved as if time travel were a possibility, and she behaved as if I were more than a dream.

So, with some trepidation, I asked, "A plan with what end in mind?"

Her blue-gray eyes widened, and she looked like a small prey animal, frozen in fear, moments from being eaten.

My heart thudded erratically in my chest.

21

BETH

I'd grabbed Edward with both hands. Physically, actually, grabbed him.

When was that? Twenty minutes ago? And I was not a physically assertive woman. Even with my exes, who I'd been very comfortable with, I hadn't ever jumped them and humped them.

Okay, I hadn't actually *humped* Edward. What we'd done was much more romantic. Very physical, but deeply intimate and romantic and sweet and really, really nice. *Really* nice. So nice that remembering it was making me warm all over.

Uh-oh. He was staring at me like I should be saying something.

Plans. Right. We were making plans. He wanted to know *what* we were planning.

I thought it was clear. We were planning *us*.

Except us included two people: me, a real life girl, and Edward, my dream guy who wasn't a dream because I was awake.

And now I was experiencing echoes of that freaky moment I experienced when I stepped into my apartment and first saw him. My world, his world, overlapping and intertwining. My mind was blown again—and I really needed to get over that. The poor man was sitting across a table from me looking like he was about to get some exceptionally bad news.

"What was the question?"

He closed his eyes, and for a brief second I could read the exasperation on his face. "A plan requires an end goal. What would ours be?"

"Um, what do you want?" I said the words, and yes, I was fully aware of how cowardly I was being to punt that question right back at him. But I'd been the one to snatch him and kiss him within an inch of his life. Except... I wasn't a coward. "Wait!"

That exasperation he'd been hiding peeked out again. To be fair, he hadn't actually been speaking when I basically hollered for him to shut it, so a little confusion, impatience, even annoyance were warranted.

I took a deep breath, and I said the words that I'm not sure I've ever uttered in my life. "I want you."

And then I realized what that sounded like and a

fiery blush to rival all fiery blushes spread across my face and then my neck. I cleared my throat, picked an innocuous spot to focus on (Edward's right earlobe seemed like a good choice, but even that small part of him was adorably handsome), and then said, "I don't mean that in a physical way."

His eyebrows climbed, but the wariness had faded and his lips were twitching slightly.

Ugh. I was officially an idiot. I'd just told the hottest man I'd ever met, the man I'd had the most chemistry with of any man I'd ever met, that I didn't find him sexually attractive. Brilliant.

"Wait, that's not what I meant. Obviously, I mean I want you in a physical way—you're incredibly handsome and I'm beyond attracted to you." At this point he was flat-out grinning, and I had to steer my gaze back to his right earlobe. "What I meant is—"

I covered my face with my hands and let loose a frustrated groan-scream.

"You want me."

Peeked between my fingers to find a satisfied smirk spread across his face. I didn't even know Edward *could* smirk. It was so very anti-Victorian. Or maybe it wasn't, because my Victorian man was definitely smirking.

And then he wasn't smirking. He wasn't anything, because he was gone.

22

BETH

Edward was gone.

Really gone.

A sick feeling churned inside me. I pressed the space above my stomach and below my heart, hoping it would fade, but it didn't.

Edward existed nowhere on the face of the planet.

This was nothing like my visits to the past. When they'd ended, I'd woken up safe in my bed.

When Edward's visit ended, he'd been yanked back to the past. And the past had already happened, which meant that right now, in present-day Austin, Edward didn't exist. Worse, he was dead.

It started with a lump in my throat I couldn't swallow past, then my eyes burned. I opened them wide and stared at nothing. If I blinked, the first tear would fall, and after that first, a river would follow.

No crying.

Crying did not lead to results.

Crying was for women who didn't have a plan.

Crying was for...me.

I bawled.

Eventually, after several hankies were dampened, a lot of snot wiped, and more sobs swallowed than I'd like to recall, a tiny seed of sanity took root. With some yoga breathing, I managed to nurture that seed and, finally, reason prevailed.

Well, as much reason as was possible when magic was involved.

I realized that whether I went back in time or Edward came forward, there was no difference in the factual circumstances: he lived there, I lived here, and what happened to his physical self during the time between those moments was not something I could dwell on.

Basically, time wasn't linear. It didn't *feel* linear. In my heart of hearts, I believed Edward was alive. I had to stop thinking of time like it was a line with a start somewhere in the infinite past and a stop at some unknown point in the future.

Edward and I had a long-distance relationship. He lived in London (1899) and I lived in Austin (the present), and while we had some complicated transportation issues, so be it. We'd work it out.

We'd work it out...with the help of a certain fairy-dust-sprinkling FG.

It was time to make a trip to Every Woman's Fairy Godmother.

Seconds before I left, keys in hand, my phone rang. Hillary's name popped up on the screen, so I answered immediately. I didn't even blink at the fact that I'd have sent a client to voice mail. I was allowed to prioritize my personal life once every decade or so.

"Hey, Hills."

"What's wrong?"

Good grief. Did she have mind-reading powers or what?

"You sound all stuffy and hoarse."

I'd spoken, what, two words? I muted my phone, cleared my throat, unmuted and said, "I haven't a clue what you mean."

"Ohmigod, you've been crying!"

"Maybe I'm coming down with something. Stress lowers the immune system and I've had enough stress to last a lifetime recently. You should know. You've been holding my hand through it all."

"You skinny blonde girl, I saw you like an hour ago. You weren't getting sick then. Quit lying. What's wrong?"

And since I knew she wouldn't stop pushing, I told her. I even managed not to sniff or get remotely teary while I went through the whole "Edward's basically dead" spiel.

"It's ridiculous, I know."

"Aw, honey. It's completely irrational, yes, but it's not ridiculous. You're worried about losing the man you love."

When she mentioned the L word, my mind stuttered and I did a teensy mental screech of shock. Surprise. Dismay. Doubt. Wonder. So many emotions.

Hillary groaned. "Wow. Let me get some earplugs."

All right, not so mental and not so teensy. "I'm not in love. Edward's...he's...you know... he's..."

"Girl, if you say he's a figment of your imagination, I'll get in my car, drive over there, and murder your filing system."

I had visions of her emptying out my filing cabinets and rearranging all the backup hard copies of my clients' work and my invoices and expensing receipts for the last seven years. There were palpitations, and I owned it. "Hey. Don't threaten the organizational foundation of my business. That's just mean. Also, you've had too many whiskeys to drive."

"How do you know that? Never mind, you're

totally right. I was bluffing. I'll actually call a ride share."

Our entire ridiculous conversation had given me the necessary time to step away from the panic ledge. I felt almost normal. Five-espresso normal, but normal. "I told him I wanted him."

And this was how much Hillary loves me and knows me. My sex-obsessed friend didn't go there. She understood exactly what that meant. "Aww. I'm wiping away tears right now, just so you know. You're all grown up, with your almost-expression of almost-affection. Just a teensy tiny step further and you'll be all the way there."

"Are you seriously giving me heck about my inability to commit right now? You were a bigger commitment-phobe than... Ugh. I don't even know who to compare you to. You were that big a commitment-phobe."

Hillary laughed. Rich, deep, rolling laughter. When she'd quieted, she sniffed, and I could tell that this time she actually was wiping away tears—of laughter. "You don't have commitment issues. You're white-picket-fence girl. You can't give me grief over those particular issues, because I've always owned them. Owned 'em and smashed 'em with a baseball bat. No, honey. You have a hard time recognizing what you want and going for it. And you went for it! Well, you mostly went for it."

A big grin stretched across my face. "Yeah, I did." And it had felt darn good. "But love, Hillary? That's huge. And our future is crazy uncertain right now. It's a scary thought."

"Yeah, it is. So what are you going to do about it?"

"Excellent question. I was just on my way out the door."

23

BETH

I arrived at Every Woman's Fairy Godmother to a closed sign.

Not the regular, after-hours version of a closed sign. Nope. There was a note. Madeleine was away unexpectedly for a family emergency but expected to return within the next few days.

A "family emergency" my tush.

When I'd been on the phone with Hillary, she tried to warn me. She told me Madeleine was only allowed to interfere so much and that after that, it was up the humans to sort their lives out. She hadn't said my supposed fairy godmother would disappear off the face of the planet.

Small problem with Madeleine's absence: I needed her dubious magic powers if I ever wanted to see my man again.

I had no fairy dust, no time travel machine, and no plan.

On the bright side, it looked like I was making strides in accepting the fact that feelings were involved. Maybe not strides, maybe baby steps.

I admitted to myself *and* to Edward that I wanted him in my life—that I wanted *him*—and now I was thinking about him as mine. I'd never been that proprietary about a guy before, including with the men I'd actually been in relationships with.

The big L word was still freaking me out, but in my heart of hearts, I knew...was mostly sure... guessed that love was lurking.

Why did my love lurk? Shouldn't it be bursting forth? Shouldn't it be a certainty and not a maybe? Shouldn't I know, without any reservation at all, that I was in love if I was actually in love?

"Beth?" I flinched, because no one liked to be interrupted while soul-searching in front of a closed vintage clothing store that *should* house a meddling fairy godmother, but *didn't* because she had a "family emergency." When I turned, I discovered a woman I didn't know waving at me. "Hi?"

Why was this person intruding on my crisis? My very personal crisis? I squinted at her. She didn't look familiar. She looked like a soccer mom. Scratch that, a soccer mom's older sister, because the sleek bob I'd thought was a bright silvery blonde from a distance proved to be silver when she got closer.

"Hi! I'm Mary Margaret." She extended her hand, as if it was completely normal to walk up to a stranger and introduce herself.

Wait, that name rang a bell. I shook her hand, but couldn't shake my confusion.

"Hillary sent me."

Aha. *That* Mary Margaret. "Um, hi. I'm not sure what exactly she was thinking you could do, but, ah, thank you." Because as annoyed as I might be, it would be impolite to point out to the psychic that I didn't believe in psychics.

"She was thinking you needed backup, and she had an appointment she couldn't miss this evening." A huge smile spread across the woman's face. "She was also thinking that I love a good love story, especially if it involves magic."

And yet another person who was team fairy dust and unicorns. I'd like to see a statistical breakdown of magic-believers versus nonbelievers in the greater Austin area. Did we have a higher ratio of woo woo folks in this geographic region? Or did I just know most of them?

"I don't know how much Hillary told you, but Edward's disappeared, and now my only lead has also evaporated into thin air."

Mary Margaret read the sign. "But it says here she's had a family emergency. I'm sure she'll be back once it's sorted."

I crossed my arms and arched an eyebrow.

"Yes, it does seem like suspicious timing, but that's the nature of emergencies: they crop up unexpectedly at inconvenient times." She examined me head to toe, but then closed her eyes and shook her head. When she opened them, she flashed me a bright smile. "Let's get coffee."

"Did you just..." I didn't know what to call what she did, something about reading energy.

"Read your aura?" She wrinkled her nose. "Only a little peek, and it was sort of by accident. I usually ask first, I promise."

I swallowed a sigh. As if my intimate thoughts hadn't had enough examination already. But I knew Hillary and Mary Margaret were both trying to be helpful, and I needed to regroup anyway. "Sure, let's grab coffee."

After a short chat, we'd decided to skip a more popular location for a quieter spot a little farther away. Ten minutes later, we sat in a corner of the local coffee joint with our steaming herbal teas.

Mary Margaret blew on her tea. "We can just chat about whatever. Sometimes talking, even if it's about something unrelated, can help relieve stress."

In for a penny, as the saying goes, so I

recounted the nuts and bolts of my and Edward's story. She knew about Madeleine, because she'd helped Hillary and Brad solve their own magical dilemma. She also knew I was basically dating a Victorian man from 1899, because Hillary had to give her some background before sending her to intercept me at Every Woman's Fairy Godmother. I filled in the rest...*most* of the rest. I left the steamy bits out.

"And here I am, with a complicated situation, lots of feelings, and no way to reach out to the person I really need to speak with." I meant Edward, not Madeleine, and I was pretty sure Mary Margaret understood that even though I couldn't seem to say it out loud.

She blew on her tea, and I could see her processing all of the pieces of my sad tale.

"You saw something, didn't you?" I asked. "When you snuck a peek at my aura before, in front of Madeleine's shop, you saw something."

"I saw something; I saw your aura." She quirked an eyebrow. "But I thought you didn't believe in such things. Hillary warned me you might not be entirely on board with my particular kind of talent."

"Ever since the first dream I had with Edward, I've been teetering between wanting to believe someone with magical powers is on my side and an inability to let go of reason."

"Your first dream *with* Edward? Not about him." She smiled.

"Oh, I know. I've officially boarded the crazy train, right along with you, Brad, Hills, and Walter." I winced when I realized exactly what I'd said. "I'm sorry. I really don't mean to be so rude, it's just such a big shift, going from fairy tales as fiction one day to fairy godmothers as reality the next. And auras, naturally."

"No offense. It is a little crazy. Not in the mentally ill sense, just in the sense that it's a departure from mainstream cultural norms. I get it. The first time I saw an aura..." She inhaled a deep breath and shook her head. "But that's a story for another time. We're here to talk about *your* story. Would you like me to have a look? Officially and more than just a peek?"

I scanned the little store. It was still just as quiet. "I guess—if here's okay?"

She nodded. She wrapped her hands around her mug, blinked a few times, and then smiled. "Okay. Tell me about Edward."

That was easy enough. We chatted about the hottest, kindest guy I knew, the only guy who got me (even though he lived more than a few time zones away), for several minutes. I definitely gushed in a girly gushy kind of way.

"I decided to treat this as a long-distance relationship, because in my head that made it better somehow."

Mary Margaret didn't crack a smile at my silliness, just nodded sympathetically. "I can see how it would. But long-distance relationships typically involve Skype calls and plane tickets."

"Exactly. I think I went a little astray there. Thinking about Edward as my English boyfriend made it easier for me to accept that he's a real guy, not some figment of my imagination, but it also made it really clear that we could never have a real relationship, because no Skype and no plane tickets could ever bridge that distance."

Yeah, I totally called Edward my boyfriend. Out loud, to another person. And he and I hadn't even had The Talk yet. I was so far gone on this guy.

"And all these months, you've both continued to appear to each other with some regularity?" she asked.

"Well, sort of. More time passes for Edward between each of my visits. From my perspective, it's all happened over a shorter time frame than for him. I guess time travel is weird that way?"

Mary Margaret tapped a finger to her lips. "Maybe."

When she didn't elaborate, I said, "What are you thinking?"

"You know that saying, you're only given as much

to bear as you're able?" She grimaced. "I can see from the look on your face that you're as much a fan of that saying as I am. But I think it might apply here. Edward didn't need to see you as often to fall in love. Maybe his heart was more open to love than yours."

"You can't know that." My denial was instant, because...just because.

"Which part?" she asked. "That he fell madly in love with you, or that it didn't take him very long to get there?"

"You can't know he loves me."

"Oh, yes. I have no doubt he loves you. Every part of your story points to it." She tipped her head and grinned. "I also have great faith in Madeleine's matchmaking skills."

"Hmm."

"That man has accepted time travel as a reality, didn't blink at showing up in your apartment clad in scandalous clothing, and makes you feel like a queen. Trust me, he's head over heels."

I flushed, but I wasn't embarrassed. The warmth on my face echoed through the rest of my body and settled right into my chest, near my heart.

"I don't think I'm telling you anything you don't already know."

I hugged my arms tight around my body. She wasn't, but why was it so hard for me to trust that something good—something wonderful—was happening?

Maybe because I was terrified, and not just for all the usual reasons: he might not be as invested in me as I am in him; he doesn't know the real me, and if he did he wouldn't like me nearly so much.

My fear with Edward went well beyond my usual fears. "How will we ever be able to be together?"

"Magic."

"But how does magic work? What buttons do I push to make it work?"

"Oh, honey. That's not a question I can answer. What can you control? That's what you need to be thinking about right now. What can you control, how can you help yourself, and that's what you focus on. Worrying about the things you can't control will drive you crazy—and this time I mean the bad kind of crazy."

We chatted a little longer, but not about anything of any consequence—her weekly tennis match, my favorite place to eat Thai, our shared love of funny cat memes. She must have intuited that I needed a little time to consider what she'd said. Accepting a lack of control over the most important aspect of my life wasn't going to be easy for me.

Only after she left did I realize she'd never told me what she saw in my aura. She'd looked, and then she'd asked me to tell her all about Edward.

I groaned, because I was an idiot. I knew exactly what she'd seen.

She'd seen my love for Edward.

As much as she might have talked about him being head over heels for me, I was completely, with every bit of my sad, terrified heart, in love with him.

24

EDWARD

The last words to leave my lips—*you want me*—rang in my head.

Arrogant, perhaps, but true.

She did want me. More than that, she loved me.

She might not be able to say the words, but I knew it. Her feelings shone in her eyes, hid in words unspoken but hinted at, and resonated through her actions.

I loved her.

She loved me.

One question remained: what was I going to do about it?

I gave myself a week. One week to visit those few people who remained in my life, to wander my favorite parks, to tie up loose ends. After that, I planned for a life in the future.

I could tell Beth I loved her—and I would—but I needed to show her, as well, and I only knew one way to do that.

I hoped for the opportunity to join her, planned as if it would happen, and would be ready when it did.

25

BETH

My heart tangled itself into knots as I drove home from the coffee shop.

I had so many feelings, and processing them was going to take some time. Fear, uncertainty, affection, passion, and love. So much love.

Good emotions swirled around next to the less good ones, and I tried—really tried, because I was normally an excellent driver—to put them aside and get myself safely home.

I think I was doing an okay job. The guy who honked at me when I failed to go on green and the lady who flipped me the bird when I got a little too close to her bumper might disagree, but all things considered, I did pretty good. But I was relieved to get home.

Relieved, right up until I put my trusty Corolla in park, because that's when Edward appeared in the passenger seat.

Time? Who needed time?

But then I had to go and doubt myself, because I'd just seen him. It was too soon for him to be here again. I was daydreaming. I must be.

My eyes fluttered shut. Maybe I hadn't handled the drive home quite as well as I'd thought.

"Beth."

Okay, maybe not a daydream. I opened my eyes—and he was still there.

The space inside my car shrank to a quarter its normal size, or that's what it felt like. I wasn't used to having passengers, especially big male passengers, and definitely not a big male passenger I was in love with.

"I love you."

It slipped out. I didn't plan it, wasn't even looking at him when I said it.

Dang it. I didn't even look at him when I said it!

Epic fail.

I turned to him, grasped his hand, and looking into his eyes, said once again, "I love you."

I was just putting myself out there left and right. Wow. Who knew I could be this brave? All thoughts of bravery, of anything at all except Edward, slipped away when he lifted my hand and kissed my knuckles. A soft sigh escaped my lips, because oh my gosh could he be more romantic?

"I thought you wanted me." His eyes crinkled with humor.

The insecurities I expected to surface when he didn't immediately reciprocate with those three magical words...didn't. I grinned and replied, "Also true."

A wide smile spread across his face. "I love you."

I'm not sure who leaned first or how the kiss started, only that our lips were locked. We lost our breaths together in a wild tangle of tongues. I slid my fingers through his hair, but it wasn't enough. I wanted my hands all over him.

That's where our thinking parted ways, because as I was sliding my hands down his chest—his lovely, muscular chest—he ended our kiss and leaned slightly away from me. His hand still cradled my jaw, but he had the look of a man about to say "slow down." Since I was usually the one voting to slow down in intimate situations, it was a new experience for me. Then I remembered: Victorian gentleman and PDA did not go hand in hand.

He glanced at my clothes. "How long has it been since I was last here?"

"Just a few hours." I rubbed my hand across his chest; I couldn't resist, and he seemed to enjoy it. "I have no idea how, but I'll take it. I was afraid I wouldn't see you for weeks, or—"

His fingers touched my lips, gently halting the words neither of us wanted to hear: that he might not come back at all.

Which prompted my next unplanned announcement. "You're moving in with me."

And yet another wow moment, because I didn't even ask. Look at me, being all assertive like a woman who knew exactly what she wanted.

"I am?" His eyes crinkled with good-natured humor. Good thing, because, again, Victorian gent, so hard to know how he'd take that one.

We'd discussed modern dating, not extensively, but enough for me to guess that he would be fine with a practical solution to living arrangements. Heck, I even had a tiny guest bedroom.

"Oh yes. We're going right now and having a key made. I'm in. I'm all in." I rolled down my window, and without letting go of his hand, I leaned out as far as I could and yelled, "I love Edward Stanbury! I'm all in. Do you hear that, Universe? I'm all in."

"I'm not sure if the universe heard you, but your nosy neighbor Rebecca did."

I thought he was teasing me, but then he pointed, and I saw that Rebecca had opened her window and was leaning out waving wildly at me.

Then she gave a loud congratulatory yell and hollered, "You go, girl!"

At least Rebecca was on our side.

And also Hillary and Madeleine and Walter and Mary Margaret.

Come on, Universe, get on board the love train with the rest of the gang.

Because if the universe or whatever magic was guiding our trips through time didn't get on board, I'd lose the best thing that had ever happened to me.

That couldn't happen, not when I'd just found him.

26

EDWARD

Slumber eluded me.

Beth and I talked late into the night, mostly of her time and what I could expect in the coming days, because we agreed that I would be staying. I had my doubts—as did she—but we kept our fears to ourselves. For now.

When in the wee hours of the night she offered me the small bedroom as my own, I accepted. She explained what a futon was and then showed me how to transform it from a settee into a bed.

The futon was more comfortable than I expected. It wasn't the bed that kept me awake; it was my fear.

I feared if I slept, I would be pulled back in time.

I feared I would wake and find the last day to

have been nothing more than a vivid, heart-wrenching dream.

I feared I would lose the love I'd just found.

When the sun rose, my hopes rose with it. I could not wallow in fear of what might be, only appreciate what I had and work to keep it.

I climbed from my converted bed, thanked the stars I was still in Beth's time, and ventured into her modern bathroom. I would take a shower, because I planned to conquer this time and all its oddities one small adventure at a time.

27

BETH

Edward looked tired.

He'd showered and shaved, but his eyes were red-rimmed and puffy. He'd even opted for coffee over tea this morning.

If only I'd had the courage to drag him to bed with me last night, I'd certainly have slept better with him next to me. As it was, I had terrible dreams of waking and finding him gone, and it seemed he hadn't fared much better.

"We should get you some decent tea," I declared into the silence.

Edward inhaled sharply, as if my words had startled him from a trance or the cusp of sleep. He blinked a few times, rubbed his eyes, and said, "Yes, if you have time." He finished the last of the coffee in his cup.

I had time. I was taking a few days off. I could do that; I worked for myself and my clients were all currently very, very happy. The perks of being a workaholic.

After we'd both finished our morning caffeine fixes, we spent a few subdued minutes tidying up in the kitchen. It had been a pleasant surprise the previous evening to find that Edward was as tidy as me and excited to learn how the dishwasher and garbage disposal functioned. He'd been equally fascinated with the concept of recycling and had dug through my recycle bin to get an idea of what items shouldn't be thrown in the trash.

He treated each new discovery as an opportunity and not as an obstacle, which only made my heart flutter all the more for him.

I hooked my arm through his. "Come on. Let me show you the joys of modern grocery shopping."

He brightened at the prospect, which in turn buoyed my own spirits. We'd also need to stop and pick up some clothes, because...well, because he was staying and he needed more than the clothes on his back. But I'd simply stop on the way to the grocery without making a big fuss. I suspected Edward wouldn't be too terribly excited about me paying for anything more than food.

When Edward opened the car door, he paused

then leaned down and picked up something that had fallen down the side of the seat.

He lifted a leather wallet I'd never seen before, then climbed into the passenger seat.

"That's not mine." As I backed out, I said, "There should be some cards inside that have the owner's name on them." And then I tried to remember the last time I'd had someone in my car who might have lost a wallet.

Silence followed.

Once I was on the road and in no danger of hitting other parked cars, I glanced at Edward. He held a driver's license in his hand and was inspecting it with complete fascination.

"What did you find?"

"Can you stop for a moment?"

I pulled to the side of the road.

"It has my picture on it and my name." He handed me what looked like a valid Texas driver's license.

I scanned the information and snorted.

"Apparently we live together and your middle name is Zephyrin." It was a little funny. Freaky as heck, but a little funny.

"That is my middle name, and we do live together." He retrieved the card, and a smile tugged at his lips. "Am I to understand that I am properly licensed to drive your car?"

"Zephyrin?"

His silence spoke volumes. How did the same people who thought Edward was a good name for their child land on Zephyrin? I sensed a story.

"We'll get back to that, but to answer your question about driving, yes, the State of Texas has licensed you to drive any car, not just mine. But you're not getting behind the wheel of my baby until you've had lessons." I patted the Corolla's dash affectionately. She might be a little older, but she was paid for and I adored her. *Newbie drivers, stay away.*

"How is this possible?" He lifted the license by the corner.

"Madeleine. It has to be." The wallet was open on his lap, and I saw other cards peeking out of the pockets. "Do you mind?" I asked, indicating the wallet.

He handed it over and then continued to examine the license in his hand. "I'm an organ donor. What does that mean?"

Yeah, that would be creepy to read if you came from a time after *Frankenstein* was published but before transplant operations. I briefly explained the concept, and he chewed on that bit of information while I flipped through the cards in what was apparently his wallet.

"You're a member of a local rowing club. Do you row?"

"Hm?" He looked up from the license for a heartbeat. "I competed in single sculls at university. So with a death, another life can be saved by recycling parts of the body?"

An interesting way to look at organ donation, but we had just discussed recycling yesterday evening. "Basically, yes. So...single sculls?"

"One man, two oars. I still practice when the weather permits." He tapped the license on his leg. "Science is fascinating."

And the mystery of Edward's stellar physique was solved. Apparently, I had a thing for rowers, scullers, whatever. Yum.

I flipped through the remaining items: a loyalty card for a fancy local tea store, another loyalty card for an Indian restaurant, a dry cleaning ticket, and a business card for a fancy barber.

It was like a smorgasbord of Edward trivia trapped in a little leather container. And with each item, hope grew in my heart that he was here to stay.

"Let me guess, you like Indian food."

He perked up noticeably. Apparently, Indian cuisine rivaled organ donation in its ability to capture his attention. "Is Indian food on the menu for later?"

"It can be. It looks like this belongs to you," I returned the wallet to him after replacing all the cards. "And we also have a to-do list for the day.

Would you like to pick up your clothes from the dry cleaner first, check out your rowing club, or buy some tea?"

"I have clothes at the cleaner?" He seemed fascinated by the prospect, so that's what we settled on.

I programmed the address into my phone, and after I pulled onto the road again, I said, "So, Zephyrin? That doesn't sound very British."

"Zephyrin was the name of a distant cousin on my mother's side, a distant *American* cousin. He was wealthy and had no direct heir." His voice was tinged with amusement when he added, "My parents were ever hopeful, hence Zephyrin."

I snorted. "How did that work out?"

"Quite nicely. He did, in fact, leave the entirety of his estate to me and another cousin with equally enterprising parents."

Which made me smile, in part because the whole story seemed very British and very Victorian while it wasn't really at all. But I also smiled because I was with Edward and we were about to spend the day together.

And then my smile grew exponentially when Edward clutched the armrest as if his life depended on it. I was driving twenty-seven miles an hour.

28

BETH

Two weeks with Edward!

I wanted to throw a party, dance a jig, sing a ridiculous song, celebrate in some over-the-top fashion. I'd always found couples who celebrated oddly timed anniversaries a little kooky, but now I got it. I wanted to celebrate our two-week anniversary.

I still panicked occasionally when Edward was out of my sight for any noticeable length of time. I wasn't clingy by nature, but these were exceptional circumstances. Exceptional, magically charged circumstances, so I definitely got a pass for being anxious.

We'd settled into a routine. He moved into my room within a few days, mostly because neither of us could sleep with the other absent.

When Edward got up, he rowed or walked. Since I knew how long he'd be gone and he had a cell phone, I didn't find myself fearing the worst during his morning outings. When he got home, we drove by Every Woman's Fairy Godmother. Madeleine's family emergency had turned into a lengthy closure of the store. Two weeks was a long time to completely shut the shop down. On the bright side, there was a coffee shop around the corner that served an Edward-approved tea, and as our daily consolation, I splurged on their fabulous croissants while Edward got a decent cup of tea.

Once home, we'd gotten into the routine of working at the kitchen table together. Edward sketched while I did client work.

I had no idea that he was such an amazing artist. I'd seen his sketch pad, of course, but he hadn't ever shared it with me. Not that he'd been secretive of the contents or shy about his work, but simply because our time was always limited and I don't think it even occurred to him.

But then we'd brainstormed a list of his skills, hoping to find something he could parlay into a profession or even a temporary job, and drawing had made the list.

He'd explained how he drew pictures of all the plants and animals he encountered on his walks. Victorian naturalists frequently documented their findings in this way, and Edward had a particular talent for realistic artwork.

He was working on a commission project now. Earning peanuts, but also building his portfolio. Despite the low pay, he'd been thrilled someone (several someones, in fact) was willing to pay him to do something he loved so much.

I watched as he colored in a lifelike and yet beautifully whimsical bunny he'd sketched earlier. "What is that one for?"

He glanced up with an adorable crinkle in between his eyes—his thinking face—but relaxed and smiled when he caught my eye. "A children's author wanted me to mock up a few different rabbits. If she likes one, then she'll be commissioning me for all of the art for the book, and possibly the series."

I leaned back in my chair, taken aback. "Really? Why didn't you mention that before?" My heart warmed that he was already seeing some success.

He fit—into my life, this world, and most importantly my heart. I loved that he was finding his place.

"I didn't want to until I was fairly sure it would work out, but she seems happy so far and I think the chances are good."

Before I could tell him how proud I was of him, the front door buzzer rang.

Edward was on his feet before I'd even clicked

save on my document. He picked up the phone for the intercom system and said, "I'll be right down."

"We aren't expecting any packages, are we?" The first week I'd ordered a few items, and that had also been an experience. Shopping on the internet, global shipping, those had been fun conversations.

"Be right back," was the only response I got.

I headed to the door and waited there as Edward ran downstairs. My curiosity was well and truly piqued, because he was being a little evasive. I sensed a plot, which had me wondering what terrifying object on the internet had reeled him in. He had a bank account and a debit card, so the sky (and his thus far miniscule bank balance) were his only limits.

He jogged up the stairs, slowing only when he saw I was waiting at the door.

"It's for me. I'll just open it later, after I'm done with this illustration." Then he laid the large, thick padded envelope on the table.

"Okay." A little odd, but I didn't think much of it...until I returned from a quick coffee break later that afternoon and found the envelope gone and Edward on one knee.

"Marry me."

I blinked at him, shocked completely into silence.

"I love you. I want to spend the rest of my life loving you. Marry me."

He went all blurry for a second, and then he stood and wrapped his arms around me. "Proposing wasn't supposed to make you cry."

"I'm not crying." A statement that I followed with an indelicate, watery sniff.

He tucked my head closer to his shoulder. "I should have planned something more romantic, but I didn't want to wait a moment longer."

I shoved at his chest and he let me go just enough that I could lean back and look him in the eyes. "There is nothing more romantic than being asked to marry the man I love. I love you. The answer is yes. Yes, Edward Stanbury, I'll marry you."

I kissed the corner of his lips, then the other corner, but when I moved in for a full-on, I'm-so-in-love-with-you, proper kiss, he said, "So you don't want to see the ring?"

There was a ring? Sheepishly, I said, "I missed the ring. I'm sorry."

"That was the only romantic part of the proposal. You missed the best part." There was a twinkle in his eyes.

"Well, no. *You're* the best part, always."

He took my hand and slipped the ring on my finger. It was a beautiful old-fashioned ring, a large sapphire surrounded by diamonds. "It was my mother's ring."

His mother's—"How in the world..."

"I made arrangements with a well-established bank and a highly-respected solicitor's office, but there was an element of risk."

"You made arrangements... You did this before, when you were in London, in the past?"

"Yes. The ring, your bracelet—"

"Madeleine's bracelet," I corrected, because it had only ever been loaned to me.

He nodded. "Also a few other items, but I'm still waiting to determine whether those plans will come to fruition."

"Wow." He'd literally gone back in time for the ring he proposed with. A ring that obviously had some sentimental value. I lifted my hand and watched the sun sparkle on the stones. "You win. The ring is definitely romantic, but I still say you're the best part."

Only one thing marred what would otherwise be a perfect moment. The same thing that had brought us together could also pull us apart: magic.

And without Madeleine, there was no assurance that Edward wouldn't be ripped away from me and deposited in a past where he no longer belonged.

29

MADELEINE

Stupid Council of FGs.

Stupid Society for the Study of Occult and Paranormal Phenomena.

Stupid governing bodies in general. Why were there so many stinking rules?

So, I tinkered a little above and beyond the normal parameters of an FG? The sky wouldn't fall just because I took a more active role in my clients' lives.

Unfortunately, my bosses didn't agree, and worse, my "excessive magical activities" had put me on the radar of the local paranormal community, governed by the Society for the Study of Occult and Paranormal Phenomena, aka the Society.

Fairy godmothers didn't mingle with the "common" paranormal crowd. That was the FG company line. Personally, I had nothing against wizards, golems, vampires, and the like.

Hmm.

Actually, wizard magic could get a bit creepy, and golems were basically a prettier version of Frankenstein's creature.

And then there were vampires. Most of them had sociopathic tendencies.

Okay, maybe I was a little snobbish when it came to paranormals. But it wasn't like they exactly opened their arms for us FGs. I was pretty sure they were partially to blame for the FG tutu and glitter rap.

We thought paranormals were a little grimy. They thought FGs farted sparkles and rainbows. Never the twain shall meet...usually. And that mostly held true. We did our thing in the shadows. They did their thing in the shadows. But our shadows didn't cross...until a certain youthful FG sprinkled too much fairy dust around and showed up on the Society's radar.

Whatever. I stood by my choices. Just because time travel left streaks of magic floating around for every wizard, witch, and vamp to see didn't mean it was a bad idea.

Magic was never wrong when used in the pursuit

of the greater good...right? And what was a greater good than True Love?

That was the gist of the pep talk I gave myself as I opened up Every Woman's Fairy Godmother for the first time in two weeks.

"I'm sorry I've neglected you, sweetheart." I patted the doorframe as I walked through the front door.

A store wasn't a living being, but there was an energy that a place developed over time, and Every Woman's Fairy Godmother had amazing energy. Warm and welcoming, soothing, comfortable. This shop had become my second home.

I sighed. As happy as I was to be back in my home away from home, the shop was also a business, and I had a lot of work to do to get caught up. I retrieved the cell phone I used solely for the store. It was dead, of course. I hadn't planned to be gone for two weeks, but the FG Council had taken more persuading than expected. They'd wanted to ground me, which wasn't an option.

First, I wasn't a child. Second, I was already on probation for something that shouldn't even be a punishable offense. And third, I was in the midst of nurturing True Love.

True Love could be a delicate, temperamental flower.

I plugged in the store cell, turned on the speaker, and grabbed a pen.

After listening to a dozen messages—three from Hillary, seven from Beth, and two from Brad—my ears were burning.

I revised my thoughts on True Love. Not so much a delicate flower as a raging, angry beast.

30

BETH

Edward and I celebrated our engagement like any madly-in-love couple would: we partied like rock stars with our closest friends until the wee hours, then spent the rest of the night wrapped in each other's arms.

Hillary and Brad had stuck around the longest. We'd finally kicked them out around three in the morning so we could get to the good stuff.

As a result, neither of us was in a state of mind to receive guests the following morning.

Hence my dismay when the door buzzer rang. At least it wasn't Hillary pounding on my apartment door. She always found a way to sneak past the security door on the first floor. A door buzzer I could ignore.

But then it rang a second time, and then a third.

Edward groaned. I patted his shoulder, because as much of a morning person as he was with all his rowing and whatnot, he was a bear when he didn't get enough sleep.

He was a complete softie, but he was well over six feet, muscular, and looked pretty disreputable this morning with his unshaven face and wild hair. I didn't want him scaring the neighbors or the poor delivery guy.

"I'll get it." I kissed his stubbly cheek, but he was already falling asleep again.

Even his imperfections were perfect. He was an adorable grump.

I grabbed a robe and slipped it on as I opened my apartment door—but I didn't get far, because Madeleine stood directly in front of me.

"Whoa. How did you get...ah, never mind." Because magic, that's how she got past the security door. "Ohmigod, it's bad news, isn't it?"

Because she'd been avoiding me, Edward, and Hillary for two weeks now. Even easygoing Brad had called a few times and left her a heated voicemail or two.

"Do you always assume the worst?" she asked.

She had a curious expression on her face, not a look of doom and gloom. And what was perhaps a better indicator of the situation, she was holding out a wrapped gift. She smiled and handed it to me. "Congratulations."

I blinked and didn't take it, because magic.

She shoved the gift at me. "It won't bite."

Edward's familiar woodsy scent filled my nose and then he wrapped a comforting arm around my shoulders. I'd have sworn he was completely passed out only two minutes previous.

With a reassuring squeeze, he said, "You can understand our reservations right now."

Madeleine frowned. "No, not really."

We both looked at her as if she'd lost her mind, because she'd lost her mind. We'd been living on the edge for two weeks, waiting for the other shoe to drop. The time-travel, I'll-never-see-the-love-of-my-life-again shoe.

Sort of.

For the first week. Definitely the first few days.

But when I thought about it, we'd actually settled into our life together much more smoothly than a lot of couples I knew. Couples who'd met under much more normal circumstances.

And then there was the wallet.

That wallet held Edward's driver's license, a legal form of ID that made so many things fall into place, including: opening his own checking and saving accounts, posting his availability on several freelance sites, and being added to my lease.

That wallet had also held a loyalty card to an Indian restaurant, which had seemed trivial at the time, but it turned out that food was about more than sustenance. Edward kept asking to go back to that restaurant, and we ate there every day for five days. A few days ago, he fessed up that while he wasn't exactly homesick, eating familiar food made him feel less like a foreigner in a new land. Indian food, of all things. Who would have thought an English Victorian guy would need Indian food to feel at home in Texas?

There'd also been the dry-cleaning ticket. When we'd arrived, the man at the counter handed over a selection of clothes that covered all the basics. I knew how much Edward hated relying on my money, and while it might have simply been a question of pride, I appreciated that Madeleine had given so much thought to his feelings.

And then there was the rowing club membership. Edward had made friends there. People who shared his interests and seemed like genuinely good people. I knew how important it was for him to commune with nature (though he'd laugh if he heard me describe it that way) and how much exercise impacted his mood. He was a lot happier when he was active. I wasn't that way, but I understood.

Madeleine had done that for him. She had done all of that to make his life here easier. To make him feel like he belonged in this world. In my world. In the present.

Wow. I was an idiot.

All of those thoughts and the resulting conclusion—that Edward was here and he wasn't going anywhere—flew through my head in seconds.

Madeleine did so much for us. Took the time to truly know us, matched us, and then made the beginning of life together possible. I was going to bawl.

Nope, too late. I was bawling.

I took the present, handed it to Edward, then tugged Madeleine in for a hug. I squeezed until she squeaked.

"Sorry," I sniffled.

"Nothing to be sorry about." She patted me on the shoulder a little awkwardly, and I realized I was still hugging her, though I'd stopped trying to bruise her ribs.

"What just happened?" Edward asked.

"I'll explain later, but everything's okay. Right?" I looked at Madeleine, but I already knew the answer.

"Everything is definitely all right," she agreed.

31

MADELEINE

After spending a few minutes reassuring Edward that he wasn't going to disappear into the past—because that ship had sailed; even if he'd wanted to, there was no going back—I headed back to the shop.

I had two weeks' worth of work to catch up on. Ruffled feathers to soothe, because a few clients had been forced to use inferior sources for their short-term vintage fashion needs. Stock to acquire, because a shop as trendy and awesome as mine didn't stock itself. And bookkeeping to update, because bookkeeping always needed updating.

I patted the doorframe affectionately as I entered. "Everything will be back to normal in the beat of a besotted heart, sweetheart. Don't you worry."

Famous last words, because when I walked into the shop, everything was not normal. Not normal *at all*.

"You." It was all I could say, because my blood was boiling. That blond-haired idiot had no right to be in my shop.

"Madeleine. How are you?"

And he was sitting on my favorite stool behind *my* counter in *my* shop. He was like an invading army. He was encroaching on enemy territory. Oh, I liked that analogy, because that meant I could bash him over the head without significant negative consequences...right?

He held up a hand. "Stop. Whatever you're thinking, don't do it. I'm here at the Council's request."

And by "at the Council's request," what he really meant was that he'd schemed his way here so that he could screw up my life even more. Hadn't he already done enough?

"So, *Edgar*, why are you here? In what capacity exactly?"

If he was bothered by the name, he didn't show it. His lips twitched with amusement.

Bad. Very bad.

When Satan arrived on your doorstep smiling, nothing good could follow.

"I'm your new mentor." Then he grinned an evil, Machiavellian grin.

Okay, maybe he just grinned, but he was evil so that made all his grins evil and Machiavellian by default.

That was my story, and I was sticking to it.

I wasn't attracted to that grin or the tousled dark blond hair or the sexy shadow of scruff on his jaw or his piercing blue eyes.

Eyes that danced with humor, which had me shutting down any thoughts of attraction. He couldn't find out that I thought he was walking sex appeal. He'd never let me live it down, and he'd also gain the upper hand in whatever it was that was brewing.

Wait... "My *mentor? You?*"

No. Nooooo.

I needed to hide in the stockroom and cry. The man who'd ratted me out to the Council, the man who'd been the cause of my current probation, was now my *mentor*.

"Don't look that way, Maddie. It's not that bad."

Oh, yeah—and he was also the guy I'd had a one-night stand with ages ago. He'd rocked my world. I hadn't rocked his.

Why? Why, Universe? Why me?

EPILOGUE
EDWARD

Madeleine left Beth and I holding onto a brightly wrapped gift and so many questions.

Beth took the box from my hands and headed for the kitchen.

Trailing behind, I said, "Are you going to explain why we're not mad at Madeleine any longer?"

"The wallet. It was all in the wallet." She shook her head, still a little teary. "Let's open this before I start crying again."

I really didn't understand what had happened. We were upset with Madeleine's lack of communication and all the worry the uncertainty of our situation had caused...and then we weren't?

Beth seemed happy. Weepy, but happy. And I was here to stay.

That was what mattered most to me. With Beth by my side, I had confidence the remaining details would work themselves out, or we would work them out together.

She tore the paper off and then opened up the box. A look of confusion clouded her features.

"What is it?"

"Paperwork." She dumped out the contents on the table. A large packet of papers landed on the table followed by a velvet pouch.

I recognized that pouch. It was the same one I'd used to store a sapphire and diamond bracelet Beth had lost on our first meeting. I'd made arrangements for it to be delivered to Every Woman's Fairy Godmother at the same time I'd organized the delivery of my mother's ring to this address.

When I picked it up, it seemed heavy. I opened the drawstring, not entirely surprised to find the bracelet and a matching necklace inside. I retrieved a tiny scrap of pink paper tucked among the jewels. "Congratulations," I read aloud. "It looks like Madeleine wants you to keep these."

"Uh-huh." Beth's distracted response pulled my attention away from the jewels to find her reading a letter attached to the stack of papers.

"What is it?"

"Um, I think it's your estate." She frowned and finished scanning the letter. "Minus some pretty hefty administration costs, but...yeah, this is your estate."

And then her eyes started to tear up.

Beth wasn't a teary woman, and I was finding it distressing. I *thought* she was relieved, but it didn't make any sense. "We don't need the money. We talked about this. We have a plan. It would have been fine if this hadn't worked out."

She frowned. "You had something to do with this?" Then understanding dawned. "You worked on this before you left, at the same time you made arrangements to have your mother's ring delivered."

"I did, but it looks like my plans needed a little magic to come fully to fruition." I crossed my arms. "Do you want to tell me why you're getting so emotional over—" I glanced at the cover letter. The sum I found there wasn't exactly mind-boggling by today's standards. Helpful, but not life-altering. "Why are you getting emotional over a little money?"

She rolled her eyes. "It's not the money."

Which was even more baffling. That's what the letter and the papers clarified: the distribution of any funds remaining in a trust I'd set up in 1899.

"You're going to have to explain it to me. I don't understand." I patted myself on the back. I was "communicating."

Discussing one's feelings, concerns, and insecurities was important for a successful romantic relationship. Beth assured me of this, and so far I'd say she was spot on. It was exhausting, but also rewarding.

"The wallet, this." She tapped a finger to the stack of papers. "Madeleine did this for you."

"Yes."

"She did all this so you would be happy here, in a place so far from your home. She's trying to give you some security, some stability, to make *here* a place you can live forever."

Ah. The light was finally shining on her somewhat convoluted thinking. Beth might be brilliant in some ways, but in others she could be surprisingly dense.

"I appreciate her efforts. And yours," I added. When her eyes widened in surprise, I said, "Encouraging my friendships at the rowing club, helping me find work, to name a few."

She blinked watery eyes at me, but at least she wasn't crying. The tears were really too much. It made my heart ache to see her cry, even if the tears were happy.

"You're my home."

Well, hell. She was crying again.

I stood up and tugged her into my arms. "I love you. Where you are, that's my home."

She hugged me tight but didn't say anything.

"You understand what I'm saying?" Her head rubbed against my chest as she nodded. "But thank you for being so worried."

She nodded again. "I love you like crazy."

"I know. And I love you like home."

Read Hillary and Brad's story, Heartache in Heels, *available now! Keep reading for an excerpt from* Heartache in Heels.

EXCERPT: HEARTACHE IN HEELS (HILLARY)

My phone rang just as I was finishing up with my lunch client, a successful businesswoman who didn't have the time or patience to keep up with styles or find outfits that fit and flattered her particular body type.

Getting paid to shop was the bomb. I loved my job. Okay, I loved all of my jobs, hence my current life dilemma.

But that was a worry for another time. I tapped the ignore button and quickly wrapped up the session.

My phone rang again as I walked to my car, and this time I stopped to see who was calling. I had two missed calls, both from Mary Margaret, and she was the one ringing me now. Oh, banana fudge fingers. That was not good.

I answered as I got into my car. "What's happened? Did Gramps freak out? Is he okay?" When she didn't answer right away, I said, "Are *you* okay?"

Mary Margaret's voice came across thin and reedy. "Your grandfather is fine. I, however, am not. Can you come right now?"

The stones of my cat-eye sunglasses bit into my hand. I didn't even remember pulling them from my purse. I slipped them on, chucked my purse into the passenger seat, and asked, "What's happened?"

"Ahh. I'm not sure. Maybe, um—"

"No, never mind. I'm driving, quick as I can. See you in ten." I hung up the phone, and then did my best to break every speed limit as safely as possible. Mary Margaret was unflappable... normally. This was *no bueno*. Also, I really needed to learn more Spanish. I lived in Texas, for goodness' sake.

By the time I arrived at Gramps', my heart was tap-dancing in my chest. It wasn't a pleasant feeling. Not at all.

On the drive, I'd managed no fewer than five horrifying scenarios, all extremely unlikely because they involved Gramps sick or injured, and *that* Mary Margaret would have told me immediately. Also, she'd specifically said that Gramps was fine.

After slamming my car door, I raced up the

driveway as fast as my three-inch heels allowed. Don't judge. I carried flats for dog walking.

Gramps came out of the house to meet me. "Slow down, Hillary. Everything's fine. I gave your friend a whiskey, and she's doing much better now."

He looked fine. No, better than fine. He looked tickled pink.

Wait, whiskey? Mary Margaret wasn't much of a drinker, so exactly how bad was this situation? At least it wasn't 911 bad. Uh-oh. "You didn't call 911, did you?"

"Pshaw. No." Even as he dismissed my question, Gramps had a certain twinkle in his eye I didn't particularly like.

I wasn't worried anyone was bleeding...but something was up. "What did you do to Mary Margaret, Gramps? She's a nice woman."

"She's a peach. And good at her job. This one's a keeper, peanut." He paused, beaming at me, then said, "She can see Brad."

Riiight.

I grabbed Gramps by the arm and pulled him the rest of the way up the walk, my heels making a satisfying click on the pavement as I approached the house.

"Hey, now. Don't get yourself in a state. I'm coming."

"Too late. I'm already in a state. You broke my

psychic. Of course I'm upset." I followed Gramps, who'd taken the lead to open the back door, into the kitchen.

I found Mary Margaret sitting at the kitchen table. She looked a little pale and had a whiskey glass in front of her, but otherwise seemed fine. And she was busily texting on her phone. That had to be good sign. Probably. People in shock didn't text, did they?

Since she was otherwise occupied, I addressed her companion at the table, a hot guy who was quietly observing us all. "I'm sorry—who are you? And why are you here?"

And since when did Gramps start hanging out with men who looked yummy enough to take home and lock in my basement? If I had a basement...and was a creepy sex fiend who locked up hot men in my basement. Clearly, I was befuddled by his buff biceps, broad shoulders, tousled, dark hair, pretty blue eyes, and overall aw-shucks hotness. He was like Clark Kent without the glasses. I really had a thing for Clark Kent.

"Ha!" Gramps cackled. "I knew it!"

His enthusiastic hollering had me shelving my dirty thoughts for the moment.

Then I realized that the strange man was eyeing me with a ridiculous degree of surprise. Finally, he said, "You can see me?" His piercing gaze met mine. "You can see me."

My heart thudded to a stop.

Okay, probably not, but it sure as heck felt like it, because everything inside me froze and felt tight, like a giant was squeezing me in his big fist.

I might be having a panic attack. Or something.

Probably I was losing my bananas.

Because if I wasn't mistaken, I was meeting...Brad.

I was seeing a figment of my grandfather's imagination. If that wasn't me going bananas, then...well, I didn't know what it was. And here was me not knowing that hallucinations were contagious.

I rubbed my eyes under my sunglasses, then realized I'd likely smeared my mascara and eyeliner. I closed my eyes but kept the glasses on. Brad might be a construct of my grandfather's wild imagination, but if he wasn't—if he was a real guy—then he was a serious hottie. No girl wanted to look like a psychotic raccoon when meeting an attractive man, even if that attractive man wasn't real.

Yeah, none of that made sense. Nifty. I was seeing things *and* my brain had turned to mush.

When I finally opened my eyes, Mr. Imaginary Hot Guy was still there. Except now he was standing and pointing at me.

"She can see me." He looked at Gramps with a

ridiculously large grin spreading across his face—and really, how was it possible he could look hotter? But he did.

I couldn't believe the words I was about to utter, but... "I guess you're Brad."

At his slow nod, I sank into the chair next to Mary Margaret.

She'd stopped texting and was watching Brad and me with great interest. "I've cancelled the rest of my appointments for the afternoon." Then she nudged her whiskey glass closer to me.

"Fabulous," I replied, then downed the remainder of her whiskey.

Heartache in Heels is now available for sale!

BONUS CONTENT

Sign up for my newsletter to receive release announcements, bonus materials, and a sampling of my different series. Sign up on my website: www.CateLawley.com

ABOUT THE AUTHOR

When Cate's not tapping away at her keyboard or in deep contemplation of her next fanciful writing project, she's sweeping up hairy dust bunnies and watching British mysteries.

Cate is from Austin, Texas (where many of her stories take place) but has recently migrated north to Boise, Idaho, where soup season (her favorite time of year) lasts more than two weeks.

She's worked as an attorney, a dog trainer, and in various other positions, but writer is the hands-down winner. She's thankful readers keep reading, so she can keep writing!

Cate also writes under the pen name Kate Baray.

For more information:
www.CateLawley.com
www.facebook.com/katebaray
www.bookbub.com/authors/cate-lawley

Made in the USA
Monee, IL
26 June 2021